POINT CRIME

THE EAST END MURDERS

Dead Quiet

Anne Cassidy

■SCHOLASTIC

Scholastic Children's Books,
Commonwealth House, 1-19 New Oxford Street,
London WC1A 1NU, UK
a division of Scholastic Ltd
London ~ New York ~ Toronto ~ Sydney ~ Auckland
Mexico City ~ New Delhi ~ Hong Kong

First published in the UK by Scholastic Ltd., 2000

ISBN 0 439 99832 8

Typeset by TW Typesetting, Midsomer Norton, Somerset
Printed by Cox and Wyman Ltd, Reading, Berks

10 9 8 7 6 5 4 3 2 1

Contents

1
Poison

When Melanie Tully ate the pasta that her sister had heated up for her she didn't notice the arsenic. She finished it quickly, hardly tasting anything. It was almost two o'clock and she hadn't eaten since breakfast. Beside her plate was a tall glass of Coke and she washed her meal down with it. Only moments passed before she began to feel unwell. At first, she thought it was the heat in the small kitchen, so she walked across to one of the windows and opened it. When she didn't feel any better she rubbed her hand back and forth across her chest, thinking that she'd given herself indigestion because she'd eaten so quickly.

A few seconds later she felt a gripping pain in her stomach and a blast of nausea that made the floor waver in front of her eyes. She made herself sit down on the chair and laid her head on the table just a few centimetres away from the empty plate.

Her sister, Alice, had left the room just after giving Melanie the food. There'd been an unpleasant argument, Alice said afterwards.

The arsenic had no taste or smell so Melanie hadn't noticed as she forked it up. The food had been steaming and the cheese on the top of the pasta had been bubbling. She hadn't minded. She liked her food really hot.

Alice had gone straight upstairs and put her CD player on. She hadn't heard Melanie retching over the kitchen sink. She'd only heard her heavy foot-steps on the stairs between tracks. The fact that they weren't speaking didn't stop her popping her head out of her bedroom door. She saw Melanie walking across the landing, her hand on her stomach, her skin the colour of a wax candle.

In her statements to the police Alice said she'd been worried about her sister's health. She'd offered to ring the doctor. *Leave me alone*, Melanie had said, warding off Alice's concerned face and slamming her bedroom door.

Alice said she went back into her own room and plugged her headphones into the hi-fi. She spent the next couple of hours finishing her homework. All the time she listened to her music. The head-phones were uncomfortable, she admitted, but she hadn't taken them off. It was a good compromise. She heard her music while the rest of the house was quiet. *Eventually*, she'd fallen into a light sleep on top of her duvet.

About seven-thirty, when Mrs Tully came in, the house was silent. It had unsettled her; *It was dead quiet*, she'd said, *like walking into a church*. She called out a few times and when there was no answer she went upstairs. She'd pushed the bedroom door and found it jammed against something. She'd banged on it a few times, getting herself into a temper thinking that Melanie was in a huff of some sort.

She found Alice working in her room, her headphones still on. She shouted at her and Alice stumbled up and followed her stepmother out on to the landing.

Together they edged Melanie's bedroom door open a few centimetres, enough for Mrs Tully to get her head in and look to see what was blocking it. Alice's stepmother gasped and she grabbed Alice's arm tightly, her nails digging into the teenager's skin. She pushed her shoulder at the door, pulling Alice along with her. When it was open far enough she squeezed into the room and Alice followed.

Melanie Tully was lying against the door, curled up in a foetal shape, her arms folded tightly across her stomach. The duvet had been dragged off the bed and was draped around the girl's legs.

The ambulance came quickly and the paramedics ran up the stairs two at a time. It was too late though. Melanie Tully was dead.

I first heard about the girl's death on my car radio. It had been headline news on one report, but then had slipped back a couple of items later on. I'd been driving to work, half-listening to the radio, thinking about the recent changes in my day-to-day life. My mum had recently remarried and my boyfriend had gone away.

I'd been having trouble tuning the radio in my car so I'd left it on a new twenty-four-hour news and talk station. The constant stream of chatter filled up the quiet of the car and took my mind off frequent traffic jams.

My living arrangements were largely the same as they had been before the wedding: my mum, the college lecturer, with her smart suits and classy briefcase; Gerry, the mature student, always in T-shirts and crumpled jeans; and me, Patricia, the daughter, aka Patsy, working in my uncle's private detective agency, my clothes smart or scruffy depending on my mood.

I still slept in my old room and made myself snacks in the kitchen in exactly the same way, and relaxed, often with my feet up, on the settee watching telly. Gerry and my mum were also still doing the same things; she, working on the computer or preparing meals or fussing over everyone else. Gerry was usually sitting behind a newspaper or a book, falling into frequent naps on the armchair, his hands clasped loosely over his round belly. He hadn't always been my favourite person but I had got used to him and I could see how happy my mum was.

I was stuck at a roundabout when the nine o'clock

news came on. After a couple of international stories, and something about a government minister, a female reporter with a dramatic voice came on. She sounded breathless as though she had just personally rushed into the studio with a story.

An investigation has begun in East London after a fifteen-year-old girl was found dead in her bedroom. There was no sign of a struggle and it was thought that the girl, Melanie Tully, had died of natural causes. Initial evaluation had suggested heart and respiratory failure. However, a post-mortem carried out this morning revealed arsenic poisoning. More news on this story as we get it...

This was followed by some bouncy music and an advert for a car exhaust company. I hadn't really taken it all in although the word arsenic stayed in my head for a few moments as I slowed down to let a mum with a pushchair cross the road. *Arsenic* was a funny word. It reminded me of science lessons and periodic tables; symbols that had to be learned for homework and a test the next day. It also brought to mind a dark historical period when men wore top hats and women wore long dresses; where wives and husbands died in mysterious circumstances and the word arsenic was whispered by Scotland Yard detectives.

A car horn behind me made me jump. The family had crossed and were ambling along the far pavement. In my daydream I hadn't noticed that the road in front of me was empty. I put my hand up in a gesture of apology and moved off.

I was glad that Billy, my boyfriend, hadn't been in the car with me. He would have rolled his eyes or huffed loudly and then I would have told him off about making niggling comments about my driving. But Billy hadn't been there because he'd gone abroad to work for a year. He'd left at the end of April and wouldn't be back in England for another ten months and three days. Not that I was counting.

The adverts on the radio had finished and the same female voice continued reading the news.

Detectives in the East End of London are expressing shock at the tragic death of fifteen-year-old Melanie Tully, who was poisoned on Saturday afternoon at her home in Leytonstone. They are currently interviewing family members who might be able to shed some light on this dreadful business. This is Rosa Perks bringing you up-to-date news as and when it happens...

I felt immediately irked by the smarmy voice of the reporter, her words weighed down with fake sympathy. The *dreadful business*, the *tragic death*. Did she care? Not one jot, probably.

I pulled into a parking space round the back of the shopping precinct where my uncle's office was. I looked at my watch. It was six minutes past nine. I knew that I ought to leap out of my car, walk briskly round to the entrance at the side of the shops and up the stairs to the glass door which had *Anthony Hamer Investigations Inc* painted on it.

But I couldn't be bothered.

Don't get me wrong, I wasn't desperately unhappy

with my job. It was just that I was feeling a bit trapped. I imagined my uncle Tony at that moment, sitting in his swivel chair, waiting for me to make him a nice cup of tea. All day long he would be the only person I would see. On my desk there would be a pile of mail to open and process and maybe even, if I was lucky, some phone calls to make.

There had been times when the job of being a private detective obsessed me, days when I couldn't think of anything other than the case I was working on. I'd often worked late into the evening, and once or twice all night long. I'd almost put myself in hospital a number of times, as well as putting my personal relationships on hold while sorting out the mess of other people's lives. For days or weeks the job simply took over my life, and I hadn't noticed the fact that I hardly ever met any regular people of my own age. Those I did meet were usually upset or grieving or downright dangerous.

Lately I'd begun to wonder if I was in the right career. I'd found myself scouring the Situations Vacant pages and thinking of myself as a secretary or a librarian or a financial adviser. I saw myself in the middle of a group of girls about my age chatting about clothes or make-up or even, if I was lucky, the price of petrol and the level of income tax.

The truth was I was lonely.

I thought for a moment about the radio station that I'd begun to listen to. Being a journalist sounded like a good job. Working in a newspaper office with lots of other people, or even better for some TV or radio channel. My thoughts were interrupted by the female news reporter's voice. This time it was low, serious and sombre. I rolled my eyes to no one in particular.

News has just come in that a seventeen-year-old girl is being interviewed in connection with the death of Melanie Tully, who was poisoned on Saturday afternoon at her home. Police sources say that a container for the poison, believed to be arsenic, has been found. A further statement is due to be issued later today. Unconfirmed reports say that the police are preparing a charge of murder. The time is nine-twelve and this is Rosa Perks keeping you in touch with what's happening in London…

A journalist. It wasn't just about reading stories out on the radio. It was about investigating events, uncovering the truth. In some ways it wasn't a million miles from the job I was doing. Except it was better paid and I'd be working with all sorts of other people.

With that thought my spirits rose, and I got out of the car and walked towards the office.

2
A Visitor

After work I drove straight home. My mood had definitely improved. I'd spent a lot of the day doing office paperwork for my uncle and at lunchtime I'd gone to the local library and looked up information on how to become a journalist. Just like everything else in life, it meant going to college and getting qualifications.

I wasn't put off by this. Almost two years before, I'd left school with reasonable A levels. A year later I'd almost gone to university but the job of being a detective had lured me away. Every time I got a bit fed up a new case had come along and I'd been drawn back, sucked in until nothing else was important.

I had the qualifications to go to college if I needed to. All it took was a bit of organization. Maybe I could even find a job working for a newspaper where they would give me time off to study.

I got in around six and was about to tell my mum about all my plans when I noticed a suitcase and a piece of hand luggage sitting side by side in the hall.

"Mum? Gerry?" I shouted.

"We're in here," came my mum's voice from the kitchen. The door was closed and as I got closer I could hear the sound of animated conversation. I looked back at the bags and wondered who had come. I dearly hoped that it wasn't one of Gerry's college friends who needed somewhere to stay. Putting a smile on my face I opened the kitchen door. The three of them were sitting round the table and there was an open bottle of wine in the middle.

"Look who's here!" my mum said.

My dad was sitting at the far end of the table in between Gerry and my mum. He was looking tanned and relaxed. He'd had his hair cut very short and the sides of it were almost grey. He stood up and I could see his T-shirt and shorts and very brown legs. He walked across to me and hugged me playfully.

"Patsy. Long time no see."

"Dad, what are you doing here?" I said, feeling mildly embarrassed at his show of affection in front of my mum and Gerry.

"It's a long story. Come and have some wine. I brought it all the way from Crete."

I sat down as he poured a glass of wine out.

"Are you still doing the detective stuff? Still working with that old dog, Tony?" he said, brightly, all smiles.

"Yes. Well, yes and no."

"What do you mean?" my mum said, looking quizzically at me.

"I mean I am," I said, "at the moment I am. I don't suppose I'll always be doing it."

I wasn't about to explain my plans in front of everyone. I smiled mysteriously at my mum and listened as my dad told a story about when my uncle Tony had started his detective agency. I'd heard it several times before and so had my mum, but I guess my dad was telling it for Gerry's benefit. Tony had been involved in a divorce case and followed some woman's husband, only to find the man in the arms of the wife of his ex-chief inspector. It had put him in a dilemma, my dad went on. Who was he loyal to? His ex-colleague or his fee-paying customer? Gerry didn't even have to think about it.

"The customer."

My dad laughed and patted Gerry on the shoulder in a long-lost friend kind of way. He was looking well, my dad, younger than his years. He was fit and carefully dressed, not just any pair of shorts and T-shirt, but ones with expensive labels. Around his neck was a single gold chain. Gerry looked very white and overweight beside him. He was hugging the stem of his glass of wine and looking closely at my mum's first husband.

I hadn't seen my dad for about six months. That wasn't unusual. He was a salesman and lived in Birmingham. A few times a year he came down to

London for a visit and once or twice I went up to stay with him for a few days.

I was very fond of him, but we weren't really what you'd call close. He and my mum split up when I was about five, so I don't have a strong memory of him as a father. All I know is that I saw him half-a-dozen times a year when I was a kid and a little less as I'd got older. He was more like a friend really, funny and generous, good company. His tastes were a bit cultural though, and whenever I went to stay with him he ended up dragging me round art galleries or to the theatre. I hadn't seen him in London for a very long time. Part of me wondered whether he was here because his curiosity had got the better of him, and he wanted to see Gerry and my mum together.

"Have you been on holiday?" I said.

"Sort of. I was just telling your mum and Gerry that I'm making some major life changes."

"Oh," I said, thinking of my own tiny attempts in that direction.

"I've packed in my job. I'm going to go abroad. I've bought a small hotel with a friend in Crete."

"Really?" I said, immediately picturing my dad behind a counter handing out room keys to holidaymakers.

"I've just come back from there and I'm going back in September to finalize the arrangements. We're going to spend the winter months renovating the place and then open up next spring. You're all invited of course."

"Excellent," Gerry said, filling up the wine glasses.

I looked hard at my mum's new husband. There was nothing he liked better than a freebie.

"What about your flat?"

"Gone! Sold. Everything I've got is in my bank account or those cases. I don't even have a car at the moment."

"Where are you living?"

"I'm going to stay in London for a month. I'm in a Bed and Breakfast at the moment but I'm hoping to find somewhere cheaper for a few weeks. Your mum offered to put me up but I can't impose."

I looked at my mum. She was beaming with pleasure. Her hand was lying casually on the table top and I noticed that Gerry had covered it with his.

"That reminds me," he said, looking at his watch, "I need to make a move. I'm meeting my business partner later."

The three of them spent a few minutes exchanging pleasantries. I picked up my car keys and walked out with him along the hallway.

"I'll drive you," I said.

"Finally passed your test?"

"Of course," I said, waving my hand non-chalantly, as though it had been nothing more than a formality.

I picked up my dad's small bag and he carried the case. We walked out of the house towards my black VW that was parked a few metres along the street.

"This is good," he said, putting his stuff on the

pavement and walking around the car as though he was a potential buyer.

"Yes, it was a present from Billy."

"How is he getting on?" my dad said, lifting his case and bag into the back of the car.

"Working hard. I think he's enjoying it."

That was an understatement. Billy's letters practically leapt out of their envelopes. His life was full to bursting. One day he was teaching mechanics, another he was digging a well; at other times he was involved in planning projects or renovating local rail networks. He certainly wasn't answering letters or taking telephone messages.

We drove the short distance to my dad's B and B chatting about his new hotel. It had twenty rooms and some outlying apartments. The big plan was to install a swimming pool so that the big holiday companies would be interested in using it.

I parked across the street and got out to open the back of the car. My dad took his bags and gave me another hug.

"We must go out a bit while I'm in London," he said, brightly. "I'll get some theatre tickets, or even the cinema, if you like."

"Yes," I said, giving him a little wave.

He walked up the steps of the building just as a couple of young women came out. They were linking arms and had rucksacks and maps. As my dad passed them they looked round, watching him walk up the steps. When he disappeared into the building they smiled at each other in a silly, girly kind of way and walked off.

I didn't blame them. He was an attractive man who had never had any trouble finding women. That had been the reason why his marriage to my mum had ended. As I started the car I thought back over the conversation we'd had, and realized that he hadn't once asked me about myself or what I was doing. All we'd talked about was his life and his plans. I should have felt disgruntled, but I didn't. That was my dad. It was Billy who'd summed it all up for me years before. The number one person in my dad's life was himself. It was something I'd got used to.

I took a last look at the B and B and a thought occurred to me. Billy's house was empty. Why didn't my dad stay there for a few weeks? It would air the place and give me somewhere to go if I got fed up being with the newly-weds.

I tucked the idea at the back of my head and drove off. The voices on the radio were involved in an angry debate about the new mayor of London. After a few minutes there was a serious-sounding music jingle and the local news bulletin started. The item that came after the main story was about the poisoned girl. The story was covered by the irritating female reporter that I'd heard throughout the day.

This is Rosa Perks bringing you up-to-date developments on the fifteen-year-old who was poisoned on Saturday. Post-mortem results have confirmed that

Melanie Tully died of arsenic poisoning. Police sources earlier confirmed that a seventeen-year-old girl has been helping them with their inquiries. I now understand that a charge of murder has been brought. We are not at liberty to name the girl but we can say that no one outside the family has been questioned regarding this matter...

A seventeen-year-old girl had been charged. No one outside the family had been interviewed. Did that mean that the girl had been poisoned by a member of her own family? A sister?

I felt irritated. Even though the news report had been dripping with the usual sincerity and concern it had been vague. What kind of reporting was that?

Driving along I began to imagine myself doing the job. For some reason I pictured myself in dark trousers and a black top, maybe with a close fitting hat on top of my mousy hair and glasses. I saw myself with headphones on talking into a radio microphone, a sheaf of papers in front of me with the details of my story. Then I thought of Rosa Perks and imagined what she looked like. All I had was her voice to go on. I visualized somebody with short, yellow-blonde hair and lots of gold – earrings and layers of chains around her neck, rings as well – and in between two fingers a constant cigarette. I imagined her being thin as a rake with masses of mascara and bright-red lipstick.

I couldn't have been more wrong.

3

NEWS TALK FM

I actually met Rosa Perks two weeks later.

My uncle Tony had got a phone call requesting a female operative for a few days' investigative work in the offices of the news radio station. I couldn't believe it when he told me. After days of thinking about being a journalist the job had seemed like winning an unexpected prize. I hadn't been able to hold back my delight.

"It'll just be scouring through paperwork," my uncle had said, grumpily. "Nothing exciting." His words fell like grey drizzle on my good mood.

It hadn't mattered. Even if I'd ended up looking through telephone books or files or computer data, I'd be meeting new people and getting experience of what a news radio station was like.

I was sitting in the reception area of NEWS

17

TALK FM when a tall, slim woman walked towards me. She had very black hair, the kind that had a navy blue shine off it. It was pulled sternly off her face into some kind of bun at the back. She had no make-up on that I could see and her only jewellery was a small stud in her nose. She was wearing plain black trousers and a white blouse. She'd rolled the cuffs of the blouse back, and as she held out her hand to me I noticed a tiny lace pattern tattooed around her wrist.

"Miss Kelly?" she said sharply, as though she had no time to waste.

I shook her hand and stood up, gathering my shoulder bag and jacket together. Because I expected to be in an office I'd dressed accordingly. I had a pin-striped straight skirt and matching blouse that belonged to my mother. I'd worn dark tights and a pair of black court shoes that I'd had for a number of years and hardly ever used. I'd even put make-up on and nail varnish. I felt overdressed.

"I'm Rosa Perks," she said. "You'll be working with me."

I was taken aback. Her voice sounded different off the air and her looks certainly weren't as I'd expected. Without waiting for an answer she turned and walked towards some swing doors. I followed after her, taking quick steps to catch up.

I'd expected the NEWS TALK offices to be noisy and busy, with people rushing in and out in pursuit of news stories. In fact it was all very quiet.

Just a long room with a dozen or so desks and computer terminals and what looked like a wall of giant fax machines. There were about six people at desks, and none of them looked up when we walked in. Rosa Perks gestured to a chair and I sat down nervously and pulled out a notepad and pen.

"How can I help?" I said.

"I need a dogsbody," she said, fiddling with the mouse on her computer. The screen immediately turned orange and the words EVERYONE SHOULD TALK ABOUT NEWS TALK marched from one side to the other until they filled the screen and then promptly disappeared. A second later they started marching back. I found myself momentarily mesmerized.

"Hello?" Rosa Perks said, her voice coated with sarcasm.

"I'm sorry," I said. "You were saying you wanted a dog. I mean a dogsbody. Here I am. Anything you want I can do it."

"Right," she said, her lips puckering at the corner. "What do you know about the murder of Melanie Tully?"

"The girl who was poisoned by her sister?"

"Allegedly poisoned. Alice Tully denies it."

"She's been charged by the police, I seem to remember," I said

"Yes, there was circumstantial evidence. This isn't public knowledge but I believe the container for the arsenic was found in the sister's bag. More damning is the fact that Alice's fingerprints are on it."

"Can she explain how it got there?" I said, puzzled.

"Nope. Which is one of the reasons why she's been charged. It also didn't help that she and her sister did not get on, rowed all the time."

"Most sisters row," I said, not from personal knowledge.

"True, but these two hardly ever spoke, rowed in school, in front of family and friends, etcetera, etcetera."

A row is a long way off from murder, I thought.

"So, Patsy, I'm interested in this case. I reported it when it broke and I'm following it through. I've been in touch with the family's solicitor and they're grateful for any positive input."

I nodded and she continued speaking.

"I don't know if you listen to the station, but we don't just report the news – we have a range of programmes. I'm preparing for a new slot next January called *Fighting For Justice*. This Alice Tully would make a very good subject for the programme. That's assuming she is actually innocent."

"You want me to look into it?"

"I've done a fair bit of work on it all ready." She bent down and pulled an orange file out of a drawer. "I'd carry on myself, but there's some local government intrigue I've been asked to cover. It's all a bit of a bore but I'm the only one in the office qualified to do it. That's what happens when you land yourself with a first, you see. Everyone wants you to head their investigation."

For a moment I wondered what she meant. A first? Then it clicked. A first–class honours degree. My mum had one, not that she ever mentioned it.

"*Fighting For Justice* is about people who have been accused of something, but who turn out to be innocent," she continued talking. "You know the sort of thing; a struggle against authority. Life imprisonment for something they didn't do, etcetera, etcetera."

Rosa Perks had a mildly bored tone to her voice, as though it was just another day's work. I guess for her it was. I couldn't help but feel a tingle of interest.

"I don't want to spend a lot of my time on this case. If Alice Tully ends up pleading guilty at the trial it'll have been a complete waste of my time. No, I want you to spend a few days nosing around, see if you can find out any background. Whoever murdered Melanie Tully had a reason. Find out what sort of person she was. It'll mean talking to the people she mixed with. I've done some preliminary work on it." She patted the orange folder and looked, briefly, at her watch. "Which is why I had to ask around and find an investigator who wasn't old and fat and male."

It explained why she'd got in touch with my uncle's agency. Most private investigators were ex-policemen or security experts. I didn't know of any other young women involved in detective work; in that way I was unique.

"What about the police?" I said. I was thinking about how narked they got if private investigators started following up their cases.

"Leave them to me. I've got some contacts in the local nick. They do me favours. I do the same for them. Just don't go around pretending to be a police officer. Tell people you're working for NEWS TALK – here, I'll give you a temporary identity card. People will usually talk to a journalist. They love the idea of being in the news."

She opened her desk drawer and started to fiddle about. After a moment she pulled out a name tag which she proceeded to fill in with a black felt-tip. The name P. Kelly stood out. Underneath it said, NEWS TALK REPORTER.

"Two things. One: don't go near the mum and dad. If we need to make contact with them I'll do it. We don't want to intrude on their grief. Two: only ring me if you've got something to report. I don't want to waste my time with unnecessary phone calls. We'll give it a week, OK? See what you can come up with."

Then she stood up and brushed down her trousers with her hand. The interview was over. I got up, holding my jacket, my bag, my pad and pen and my badge.

"Oh, last thing. Tomorrow afternoon, Alice Tully is coming into the office for an interview. It would be good if you could make that."

"She's on bail?" I said.

"Yes. Nice girl from a good family. She has to report to the police station every five days and has to adhere to an eight to eight curfew, but still, she's thankful she's not behind bars. You can find your own way out, can't you Patsy?"

I nodded and watched as she picked up a pad and shoved a pen behind one of her ears. Then she turned and walked through a far door. I put my bag down and attempted to sort myself out. I packed the orange folder and my pad and badge away. I spent a minute putting my jacket on, and looked over Rosa Perks' desk. It was surprisingly untidy. A grimy coffee mug sat in the middle with the name *Rosa* tippexed on the side. Beside it was a greetings card that said *Congratulations On Your Promotion!* There was no one in the area so I picked it up. Inside were a dozen or so names: *from Gloria, best wishes Mary, George, Sheila,* and so on. My mum had had cards like this when she changed her job or got a promotion. They were usually covered in little personal messages or witty jokes and there were kisses dotted around. This one just had a list of names as though someone had gone round and forced everyone to sign it.

Rosa Perks may well have a first-class honours degree, I thought, but that didn't make her popular.

I found my own way out of the office.

4
Friends and Enemies

I got into my car and drove towards the super-market in Tottenham where my friend Joey Hooper worked. Getting closer to the area I could feel this familiar sensation creeping up on me. It was a mixture of excitement and gloom. I was looking forward to our lunch but I was also uneasy about it. I had unpacked Rosa Perks' orange folder and left it on the passenger seat. I knew that Joey's lunch break wasn't for at least another half-hour so I intended to park and read through the file.

The supermarket was in what was called a "retail park" at Tottenham Hale and Joey had been working there since he'd finished his A levels. I had known Joey Hooper for about nine months. He'd been involved in a case I'd investigated. He was a young black man who'd lost his older brother in a racist attack. He'd tried for some sort of revenge and had ended up in prison himself. Since he'd got out he and I had linked up again. He was younger than me, but the experiences he'd had made him seem much older than his years. Since Billy had gone to Africa we had become firm friends.

I said the word over and over to myself. *Friends*. Joey Hooper and I were *friends*. It described how we were together. We got on, we made jokes, we talked for hours on end, we went out together. What it didn't describe was the other stuff that had recently happened. The times we spent holding each other and the long kisses that left me breathless and light-headed. The visit to the cinema when I laid my head on his shoulder, and the time I spent with him in his room, listening to records, lying beside him on the top of his bed. No, the concept of *friendship* didn't seem to cover these things.

I had a boyfriend. I wrote to him regularly and told him about most of the things that I was up to. I never lied to him. I just left out tiny bits of the truth. Was that so bad?

Joey and me first met up again a couple of months ago. Since then we'd kept contact and the physical closeness had just built up. First it was a hug or kiss on the cheek if we hadn't seen each other for a few days. Then it was a peck on the lips when I dropped him off at home. At some point, in the last couple of weeks, it developed from one kind of kiss into another. Nothing else changed. We weren't going out on *dates* together; Joey didn't act any differently to me. We were still *friends*. Except for the physical stuff.

I drove into the supermarket car park and found a space far away from the shop entrance under the shade of a giant tree. I picked up the orange folder in a businesslike way. It was a relief to have something else to think about. I pulled out the documents. The first things I looked at were two school photographs. One of each of the girls. They both looked very different, and then I remembered that they were stepsisters, not blood relatives.

Melanie Tully, the dead girl, had a small face that was framed by tight curly brown hair. It looked like the kind of hair that was difficult to manage. Her looks were unremarkable, although her smile showed a set of straight, even teeth. She had small gold stud earrings on and the knot of her school tie was loosely done. On the back of the photo were some statistics. She was five foot two; quite small, I thought. Her date of birth showed that she was fifteen, nearly sixteen. From her weight she must have been painfully thin, and she apparently had a small bluebird tattooed on her shoulder.

Her sister, Alice Tully, was a bigger girl altogether. Her face was broad and she smiled with her lips shut in an inhibited kind of way. Her hair was brown and straight, parted in the middle and down to her shoulders. It had a shine on it as though it had been polished. Her tie was tightly done up and I got the feeling she was sitting upright and straight as though she had a broomstick up the back of her shirt. Looking closely I could see a badge on her tie. I couldn't read it but it looked like the sort of thing prefects wore in my old school. The photo was a couple of years old at least. On the back of it were some listed details. She was five foot eight, much taller than Melanie. She was currently seventeen and in her first year of A levels. Rosa Perks had scribbled underneath: *Very Academic!*

I looked back at the dead girl, who looked about half the size of her stepsister. I pulled out a piece of paper on which there were some background details. I read through it and then turned over to the other side.

Melanie's mother, Susan, was a nurse and had met Alice's dad, Frank Tully, some five years or so before, when he was a patient in her ward. He had a middle management job working for a local council, and had suffered a heart attack on his way to work one morning. The couple had got married pretty quickly and bought the house in Leytonstone where they'd all lived. The new family had seemed quite a success at first. The two girls had had their own bedrooms and were in different years at school. At first they'd spent a lot of time together, but when they reached their teens some cracks started to show. The differences between them became markedly obvious. It wasn't just that they looked so unlike each other, but their personalities were almost opposite. Melanie had hated school. She had done badly in tests and had spent a good deal of her time either off sick or truanting. Alice, on the other hand, had done very well at school, getting ten GCSEs, four of them As. Melanie had been a passionate vegetarian and animal lover. She had worked on a voluntary basis at a place called Pet Sanctuary in Essex. Alice had lots of friends and when she wasn't studying went out to concerts and festivals. Alice liked to enjoy herself and worked hard so that she could do so. Rosa Perks had written, *a girl after my own heart*.

The two girls had argued over everything, their parents said, so did their school teachers and friends. Sometimes the arguments had developed into physical nastiness. Alice had had scratch marks on her arm and once had to go to casualty for a knee injury after falling down half a dozen stairs. Sue Tully, the notes said, had witnessed an incident where Alice had slapped Melanie round the face, *for absolutely no reason*, the dead girl's mother had added.

I let out a *hmm* sound. It sounded like family tensions had boiled over on many occasions.

After Melanie's body had been discovered, the police came. Rosa Perks' relations with the police must have been very good indeed because there were a whole lot of details that only the scene of crime officers would have known.

The girl had been dead for about an hour when they found her curled up behind her bedroom door. If Mrs Tully had come home from work earlier or if her sister hadn't had her headphones on the unfortunate girl might have been saved.

The arsenic had been found in the remnants of a vegetarian lasagne. There were traces of it in the dish where Alice had heated it up for her stepsister. The food had been a leftover from the previous evening when the whole family had had it. Alice had got it out at lunchtime, meaning to have some herself, but in the end she'd changed her mind. She'd skipped lunch, she said. When Melanie had come back from the Pet Sanctuary just before two o'clock they'd argued. *It was over something and nothing*, Alice had said. In an attempt to keep the peace the older girl had offered to heat the food up . After that Alice had left Melanie on her own and gone up to her room to listen to music. She'd last seen her stepsister on the landing when she'd offered to get her a doctor.

The police made a search of the house and found a small empty glass container in Alice's rucksack. Forensic tests showed that it had held a pesticide which contained arsenic. Further tests had shown a partial set of fingerprints on the glass. Those of Alice Tully. It looked like it was an open and shut case.

A knock on the window of my car made me start. Joey Hooper was bent over, looking at me covered in bits of paper and photographs. The half an hour that I was to wait had slipped by and I was only just at the end of Rosa Perks' notes. I wound the window down.

"Hi," I said, smiling.

"What's this?" he said pointing at the file.

"A case. Well, some work anyway."

"And the smart clothes?"

"I had a meeting with a journalist," I said, patting down my skirt and blouse. I'd quite forgotten how formal I looked.

"Can we go and eat?" he said, pointing at a fried chicken place at the far end of the retail park.

"Jump in," I said, pulling all the papers together and shoving them into the orange folder.

He was wearing tracksuit bottoms and an Arsenal polo shirt. His hair was very short and at the side of his head he had an H razored into it. It was one of the things I'd first noticed about him. That had been a long time ago. Just then he leant over to nuzzle the skin of my neck.

"I could eat a horse," he said, his lips on my skin.

Just friends. That was what I kept telling myself. I shook my head at my own silliness. I put the car into gear and drove off in the direction of the chicken place.

Later, on my way home from work, I dropped by Billy's house. I didn't use my key, I knocked on the door and waited. My dad, his mobile phone at his ear, let me in and beckoned me to follow him into the kitchen. All the while he talked on to the person on the other end. In the middle of the kitchen table there was a laptop computer and a pile of disks and papers.

"OK. OK," my dad said, "I'll speak to you tomorrow."

He finished his call and put his phone on the table.

"There! That's done. Tea? Coffee?"

I nodded and sat down in a chair. Even though he was indoors, working by himself, my dad was still smartly dressed; dark trousers and an open-necked shirt. He was just like my mum in that respect; even her jogging trousers and sweatshirts were carefully ironed and hung up. I was different. Getting dressed up to go out was fine, but lounging around in the house usually meant old, comfortable clothes that hadn't seen an iron for some time. It was the one thing that Gerry and I had in common.

"Are you absolutely sure Billy won't mind me staying here?" my dad said, pouring boiling water into an old teapot of Billy's that I hadn't seen used for years.

"I know he won't mind. He wanted me to move in here for the whole year he was away."

"Why didn't you?"

"I don't know," I said, truthfully, "I suppose I wanted to stay with Mum."

"That's nice. Mummy's girl," my dad said jokily.

"I do keep a key, just for emergencies," I said, holding my key-ring up, "I won't use it while you're here."

My dad waved his hand as if it didn't matter whether I did or not. He looked thoughtful, as though he had something on his mind.

"What do you make of this Gerry?"

I was stumped for a moment. My mum's new husband and I had had our differences and I hadn't always been pleased with his constant presence on my settee and in my mum's life. All the same I didn't really feel like saying anything bad about him to my dad. Don't ask me why.

"He's all right. He takes a bit of getting used to but he's OK."

My dad looked closely at me for a moment. As if he had something more to say on the matter. Then he seemed to decide against it and fiddled with the handle of his cup.

"Now that I've settled in I want you all to come round for a meal. I do a great vegetarian lasagne. Make it Wednesday. That's if your mum and Gerry are free."

"OK," I said, "I'll tell them."

He leant over and gave me a quick peck on the cheek, and I left soon afterwards.

On the passenger's seat of my car I saw the orange folder and remembered the case. *Vegetarian lasagne*. That had been the dish that Melanie Tully ate before she died. The thought gave me a little shiver so I put it out of my mind and drove home.

5

Sherman Street

The Tully family lived in Sherman Street, just off Leytonstone High Road. I drove there at about eight-thirty the next morning and parked my car about twenty metres along from their house. I wanted to have a good look at the area.

I was wearing a loose shirt over the top of some cotton trousers. With my shoulder bag and my glasses I looked quite smart, but not officious. I knew from working on past cases that the way you look is very important. It can make the difference between people talking to you or not.

I'd modelled the outfit for Gerry earlier. He'd been in the kitchen, sanding the window frame behind the sink. This was unusual. Gerry usually lived on the sofa with a pile of books at his side. I'd never seen him do any DIY before.

"That looks good, Pats," he said, puffing with exertion.

Then I showed him the T-shirt I had on underneath. It was old and had the words *Ban Fox Hunting* on it.

"I had one similar to that years ago," he said, wistfully.

I'd also grabbed a small straw sun hat off the top of my wardrobe. It was part of a collection of hats that I'd owned for years. I put it on and looked at the result.

I was pretty ordinary-looking really, not too tall, not too short. My brown hair hung about shoulder length and my glasses sometimes made me look studious. The nice thing was I could look different if I wanted to. Make-up, stylish clothes, shelving my specs; all these could make me into a completely new person. Today I wanted to look respectable but also socially conscious; I hoped it would earn some points for me when I went to the Pet Sanctuary later.

I got out of the car and buttoned the shirt up. Along the road was an old milk float, something you don't see as much as you used to. It was grimy and looked as if it had seen better days. Its engine was running and it was half-heartedly parked some way from the pavement which made it difficult for other cars to get round it. The driver, a red-faced man with a puffed-out belly, didn't seem bothered and was counting out bottles of milk from one crate to the next.

I walked up the street on the opposite side from the Tullys' house. It was full of Victorian houses that looked as though they'd been well cared for, as though they'd had money spent on them. The small gardens were carefully planted and there were climbing shrubs plaited up wooden trellises round the front doors.

The Tullys' house was no different. It was semi-detached and had a heavy wood front door with stained glass panels. At the detached side was a wooden gate which led, I knew, round to the back of the house. This had been something that Rosa Perks had underlined heavily in her notes. *Could someone have entered the house round the side and planted the poison?* she'd written.

The sound of barking dogs could be heard from the next house. I looked around to see a picture of a cute Yorkshire Terrier in the front bay window. The words *A DOG IS FOR LIFE NOT JUST FOR CHRISTMAS* were underneath it.

I turned back to the Tullys'. The side gate didn't seem to have a padlock, although it was probably bolted from the inside. It wasn't particularly high either and it didn't have barbed wire or broken glass along the top. Would it be so hard, I wondered, to climb up and over it?

"Do you want something?" A voice startled me from behind.

"Sorry?" I said, turning round.

A man of about forty was standing looking angrily

at me. His hair was steel grey and looked as though it hadn't been combed. He was wearing jogging trousers and a T-shirt and carrying a newspaper. He walked up to the gate of the house I was looking at and pushed it open with his foot. I guessed it was Frank Tully, the dead girl's stepfather.

"Haven't you lot done enough poking around?" he said.

He looked exhausted, as if he'd just run a great distance.

"I ... I..."

I started to open my bag to get out the NEWS TALK badge that I had but then I remembered that I wasn't supposed to talk to the parents. I stood with my mouth open not sure of what to do. If I turned and walked away it might seem rude but if I spoke to him it might seem like harassment.

"I'm going to make a complaint to the press association," he said, pulling a bunch of keys out and opening his front door. "You'll hear from me again!"

The front door slammed shut and my heart sank. Rosa Perks had told me not to approach the parents. I wondered whether to ring her or just ignore it and hope that the man would just forget that he'd seen me. I was pulling my car keys out as the next-door neighbour's front door opened and three Yorkshire Terrier dogs shot out, barking ferociously. They were followed by an old lady who stepped gingerly out of her porch and on to the ground. She was small and thin and looked about a hundred and ninety. She was wearing an old-fashioned apron, the kind that wrapped around covering almost all her clothes. She moved surprisingly quickly, shushing at the dogs all the while. I was on the brink of walking off but there was no one else around and I guessed that she wanted to speak to me.

"Don't be upset dear," she said, bending down to pick up one of the dogs.

Even though it was a warm day she had a hand-knitted cardigan on. The dog in her arms was straining towards me, sniffing madly in the air. I put my hand out and patted its head lightly.

"That's OK. I can understand that Mr Tully is really upset."

"Such a nice family," she said, slipping her long bony fingers into the front pocket of her apron.

"I must go," I said, keen to move off in case Frank Tully was looking through his living room at that very moment.

"My dogs like you," she said.

"Really?" I said, for politeness. I was already half-turned towards my car.

"Yes, I can tell. Usually they bark at everyone, my dear. Even my brother. They're only quiet for me."

"Right," I said, giving the dog in her arms an extra pat.

"Here," she said, holding something out to me.

Hiding my irritation I held my hand out and saw her drop a boiled sweet in it. It was in the shape of a pear. I couldn't help but smile.

"Thank you," I said.

"We all feel so terrible about what happened, dear. I was here just yards away! If only we'd known. I'm a first-aider. I could have helped."

"Yes," I said, "it's an awful waste."

I really felt like a fraud. I was making the right noises but I didn't know the girl or the family. The old lady gave a shake of the head and walked back to her front door taking the tiny dogs along with her.

As I drove away I found myself following the milk float as it glided along at a snail's pace. Once or twice I had to stop for oncoming traffic. I was staring into the back of the old vehicle, dusty and covered in grime. Someone had written the words *Clean me please* on it.

I was feeling deflated. I popped the sweet into my mouth. For all my smart clothes I hadn't made a particularly good start. I hoped it wasn't a portent of things to come.

6
The Pet Sanctuary

The Pet Sanctuary was on the edge of Epping Forest. It took about thirty minutes to get there. The establishment itself was not as grand as it sounded. It was an old house on the outskirts of Loughton, run by a woman called Wendy Smith and her son Harry. They had used some money of their own but mostly they relied on public donations. They were due to close down in a couple of months and move to new premises.

It was the old couple who lived next door to the Tullys who first told Melanie about the sanctuary. She'd visited it a couple of times and ended up as a volunteer worker at weekends. Her mum and stepdad had been delighted. Melanie's poor performance at school had got them worried and they were just glad to see that she was sticking at something.

Once in Loughton I turned left into a narrow country lane with thick trees on either side. After about a minute I came to a row of four detached houses aptly called Forest Walk. The end house held the sanctuary. I pulled my car up outside and got out. In my pocket was the NEWS TALK badge that Rosa Perks had given me. This time I was being an up-front journalist.

The other houses were in need of repair. All of them had been divided up into flats. I was surprised by the state they were in. Victorian houses on the edge of Epping Forest, just ten minutes walk from the Central Line tube, should have been worth their weight in gold. These houses had a sorry look about them, as if no one cared.

In comparison the sanctuary stood out. The windows and doors had been painted a post-box red. A neat sign over the front door announced PET SANCTUARY *Proprietor Wendy Smith. Opening times 12.00–6.00pm. Closed Christmas Day*. On each side of the front door was a giant terracotta pot full of geraniums. It was really pretty. I wondered why they were moving.

From somewhere behind the house I could hear dogs barking. I rang the bell and waited. Looking up and down the road I noted that in the time I had parked and got out of my car nothing else had passed by. It certainly was a quiet place.

The front door opened and a large blonde woman stood in front of me.

"Are you from Dixon? I've not got the time for this," she said tersely, turning and walking back down the hall and disappearing into a doorway.

My mouth was open to speak but I closed it again and took a hesitant step into a wide hallway. It was a reception area of sorts, with a line of old wooden chairs up against one of the walls.

"You'll have to give me a minute!" I heard her say so I sat down and looked at a wall of animal posters. Some of them were pretty pictures of cats, dogs and rabbits but others were advertisements for pet medicines or campaigning posters for pet charities.

"I've told Mr Dixon a dozen times that I'm not going a day before I have to."

The blonde woman came back into the hallway. She had a very round face, her cheeks puffed out and coloured with rouge. Her hair was frizzy as if she'd had a perm at some time. She wasn't what you'd call fat, but she was big, and her powder-blue trousers and top were just a little too tight. On her feet she was wearing flip-flops and her toenails were crimson. She was holding a ginger cat under her arm. It had a sad look about it, and its legs were hanging limply.

"I think there's been a misunderstanding. Are you Wendy Smith?" I said, getting my NEWS TALK card out and giving it to her. She swooped the cat from one arm to the other and took the card.

"That's me. This is Fred. He's not too well at the moment."

"I'm here on behalf of NEWS TALK. I believe someone rang and told you I'd be coming. It's about the Melanie Tully murder…"

"Poor Melanie. Why don't you come into the back?"

I followed her down the hallway.

"It's a nice place this," I said, just to be chatty. "Why are you moving?"

"It's a sore subject. The rents have gone sky high. We just can't afford to stay."

"Oh."

She took me into a long room at the back of the house. There was a strong animal smell that wasn't particularly pleasant. One wall was lined with cages, most of which seemed to house doleful-looking pets. She opened one and gently put the ginger cat in, whispering affectionately as she did it. The other wall had a sink and some kitchen cupboards.

The room was painted white and had a long wooden table down the middle. On top of it were ring-binders and piles of papers and magazines. At the far end were French doors that were open and looked out on to a long garden that also had cages and animal pens.

"It costs a fortune," she said, walking back to me, brushing her clothes down, "food, vets, staff, maintenance. When I started it was just half-a-dozen cats and dogs and me and my son. Now it's a much bigger operation."

"I can see," I said.

She stood at the table and began to leaf through a packed ring-binder. I decided to be quick. I got my pad out of my rucksack.

"Melanie first joined the sanctuary about three months ago?" I said.

"That's right. Her neighbour told her about us, she said. An oldish man, Mr White. He brought this injured stray in that he'd found up in the forest. He was so grateful that he organized a raffle at his work and raised a couple of hundred pounds for the sanctuary. We could do with more people like that. Anyway, that's how Melanie came. She just turned up one day. Skinny little thing, I felt quite sorry for her."

"What sort of worker was she?" I said.

"Terrific with the animals. Not much good with people though."

"Oh?"

"Worked her backside off when it came to anything with four legs. That's why I kept her here. Didn't mind what she did; exercising the dogs, cleaning, running errands, anything. A lot of kids who volunteer don't mind petting the animals but when it comes to cleaning out their cages or lugging around bags of feed they're not interested. Melanie didn't care. She'd get down on her hands and knees and shovel up a ton of…" she stopped.

I was scribbling frantically, wishing that I knew shorthand.

"Anyway she was very good with animals. People,

on the other hand, she didn't get on so well with. Got upset at the slightest thing. Nobody, not anybody, was allowed to drink out of her mug. She fell out with some of the staff. Mind you, she was quite friendly with Harry, my son, and his wife. But then he's a bit weird so they went well together." Wendy gave out a hearty laugh.

"Is he around?" I said, hoping he was.

"He's just popped out. He'll be back shortly."

"Did she row with anyone in particular?" I said, getting back to Melanie.

"It wasn't exactly that she rowed with people. She was very protective about her own things. Wasn't very good at sharing, if you know what I mean."

"Did she seem upset or preoccupied during the couple of weeks before she died?"

"Difficult to say. She was pretty moody most of the time. She came in every Saturday morning, did a decent day's work and then she went home. Sometimes she came in Sundays. The person she was most friendly with was Harry. And Bernice, of course, my daughter-in-law."

Wendy Smith glanced at her watch. I knew my time was up. Just then I heard the phone ringing and someone answering it from the next room.

"Wendy," a voice shouted, "it's Mr Dixon."

"Oh, damn and blast, excuse my French," Wendy said.

I listened to her flip-flops slapping on the floor as she went to take the phone call. I walked over to a cork notice board and saw a whole range of flyers stuck there. Cheap Pet Food, Pet Health Insurance, Wildlife Trusts, Beaver Sanctuary, Homes for Greyhounds. There were even some political leaflets. Against Fox Hunting, Against Fur, Against Factory Farming.

In the middle was an odd one that stood out. There was an acronym, FAST. I scanned the print and saw that it stood for *Free Animals from Slavery Today*. It was one I hadn't heard of. I'd started the first paragraph which was about animal experiments for cosmetics when I heard Wendy Smith coming back.

"That was my landlord. Not a nice man," she said, rubbing her hands together as though she'd just had a good row with someone. "Now, do you think you'll be able to put something in your report about us being forced to move out of here because of increasing costs?"

"Possibly," I said, unsure.

Rosa had arranged it so that the radio station was doing a local interest piece on the sanctuary. It had been a way to get Wendy Smith to speak to us. I wasn't actually sure what would go into the report. Before I could answer I heard the front door close and footsteps along the hallway. A young man came in, carrying a couple of cardboard boxes.

"Hi," he said cheerfully, "are you the lady reporter?"

I nodded and watched him as he put the boxes on the floor and started to unpack them.

He was in his early twenties, I'd say. His hair was about chin length and there were plaited bits hanging over his forehead. He had green combat-type trousers on and a plain white T-shirt. There were several tattoos up his arms, one of which was a small bluebird. I remembered then that Melanie Tully had had a similar one on her shoulder.

"This is my son, Harry," Wendy Smith said. "If you want any more information on the sanctuary just ask him."

I smiled as she went out of the room. I looked at my notepad and opened my mouth to speak but stopped when I saw Harry Smith staring straight at my chest. I remembered then that I had my *Ban Fox Hunting* T-shirt on. I found myself pulling my blouse across it with embarrassment. He continued looking though. His eyes were a piercing blue and he didn't even seem to blink. The sound of the door opening made him look away. A thin blonde girl in purple leggings came in. She had a short white overall on and she didn't look happy.

"There you are," she said "I've been looking for you. I'm just starting to organize the feeds," she said, looking quizzically at me.

"That's OK, we'll get out of your way. We can use my office," Harry said.

"You don't have to go," she said.

"It'll be quieter in there," he said directly to me.

I assumed it was his wife, Bernice. She looked put out and I smiled at her in what I hoped was a friendly way. Harry Smith walked out of the room without another word.

"I won't keep him long," I said, apologetically.

She shrugged and squatted down on the floor to scoop out cupfuls of dried food from a giant plastic drum. I left her to it.

Harry Smith's office was a tiny room at the back of the house. The floor was tiled as though it had previously been a scullery or a workroom of some sort. It was barely big enough for a desk and a chair. A sign on the door said OUTREACH OFFICE. He saw my puzzlement at this and explained.

"My mum runs the sanctuary and I do most of the travelling round. I go and pick up unwanted pets; sometimes I check on animals that we've rehomed."

"What about your wife? Bernice, wasn't it?"

"She helps out. That's how we met. She started as a volunteer. Have this seat," he said, taking a pile of folders off a chair and pushing it in my direction. "How about a cup of tea?"

"Yes, please. Two sugars."

He left me there and I heard him walk back up to the room we'd just left. I could hear his voice as well as his wife's but I couldn't make out what they were saying to each other. The tone was hushed and sounded like it was on the edge of anger. After a while it went silent and I heard the sound of cups chinking. I made a note on my pad about speaking to Bernice when she was on her own.

Harry Smith's desk was covered in papers and

files. There were also stacks of leaflets about the RSPCA, the PDSA, the National Trust, Guide Dogs for the Blind and several other worthy organizations. They were glossy and attractive. At the far corner were some plainer leaflets, obviously home-produced on someone's computer. One of them caught my eye. The acronym FAST was across the top. Underneath it were some photographs that made me start. A mouse with an ear growing on its back. I remembered reading about such a thing in the newspapers some time before. Beside it was a picture of a rabbit that had a lump growing on the side of its head that was the size of a golf ball. The words above it were: *Torture and Sacrifice. These and other animals suffer and die every day in the pursuit of science.*

Harry Smith came back into the room and saw me looking at the leaflet.

"Take one," he said. "The more people who know about this stuff the better."

"It's horrible, " I said, folding it up and putting it into my trouser pocket.

"Maybe you could get a T-shirt about it?" he said, with a half-smile, holding out a mug of tea.

He was making fun of me. He hadn't been taken in by my T-shirt and I suddenly felt very silly. I took the tea and decided to ignore it.

He sat down on the floor with his legs crossed, blowing across the top of his drink. I was disconcerted looking down on him. It didn't seem to be the right position for an interview. I cleared my throat and then looked at my notebook. Melanie, it seemed, had fallen out with most of the staff but had got on well with Harry. And his wife, Bernice.

"I understand you were quite friendly with Melanie?"

"Yes. She was a bit offish but I – we – liked her."

"She didn't get on with most people, your mother said."

"That's true. She got on with the animals though. She loved them. I think that shows something good in a person. She worked up here for nothing. She even spent some of her own money to buy things for the strays, treats and stuff. She was always in here asking for information about organizations and campaigns. She said she was going to work with animals when she left school. I think – me and Bernice, we think Melanie would have been good."

The door opened suddenly and Bernice's face was there. She looked quickly from Harry to me and then back again. He seemed to sigh. There was a moment of embarrassing silence so I filled it.

"You were quite friendly with Melanie, Bernice?"

"Yes. I liked her. She was nice."

There was a frozen smile on her face as she said it. The words were clipped and tight as though they'd had to squeeze out of her lips. The atmosphere was glacial.

"I ought to go," I said, gulping down a few mouthfuls of scalding hot tea.

Harry Smith stood up and placed his cup on his desk.

"I'll see you out," he said.

"Thanks for your time," I said, glancing at Bernice before I walked out into the hall. She didn't answer, just gave another forced smile. Harry walked briskly on and was almost at the front door by the time I left his office.

Out in the street a Rolls Royce had parked a few feet along from my car. It was turquoise blue and looked completely out of place. Miami or Los Angeles perhaps, but not the back lanes of Epping. Beside it, in total contrast, was an old blue van. Harry Smith took some keys out of his pocket and walked towards the van. He gave me a brief wave and proceeded to open the doors and duck into the back of the van. I turned to my car. From behind I heard Wendy Smith's voice.

"Look at him, showing off his toys," she said loudly enough for *him* and perhaps even the people down on the High Road to hear. I looked over at the car.

A middle-aged man stood by the Rolls Royce. He had cropped grey hair and was wearing a dark suit. In his hand he had a mobile phone, the type that folds open. Behind him, in the back window of the car, there was the face of a big dog. After a moment it started to bark loudly, scrabbling at the window as though it was desperate to get out. It looked downright dangerous.

"Dixon." She almost spat the word out. "He's bought these houses off the council. That's why I've got to move out!"

Mr Dixon looked up, snapped his phone shut and gave a mock salute in our direction.

Wendy Smith called him a very rude name and looking back to me added, "Excuse my French, dear."

I looked away with embarrassment. It wasn't the sort of French I remembered learning at school. I got into my car and drove off.

7

Alice Tully

The first time I saw Alice Tully she was fiddling nervously with her earrings. She, Rosa and myself were in a small private office at NEWS TALK. She had gold hoops through each ear and she kept twisting the left one round and round. I watched her for a full five minutes while Rosa Perks got the tape recorder set up and ready to go.

Rosa was looking very businesslike, talking lightly to Alice as she plugged the machine in and set it up on a table. She was wearing a black skirt and a white blouse. Her hair was pulled back again, but not in a bun this time. It was loosely tied with white ribbon. I had to admit it looked nice. Black and white seemed to be her colours.

"Why don't you have a seat, Alice?" she said cheerfully.

"I'd prefer to stand, if you don't mind," Alice Tully said, giving a shake of her long hair.

I didn't speak. Rosa had given me my instructions a while before. "I'll ask the questions. You watch her. See what her expressions are like. Listen in for the silences. They can tell you a lot about what's going on in a person's mind."

So I'd got a chair and sat down silently while Rosa fussed around the room. It gave me a chance to pull together a report of what I had done that morning. Although Rosa didn't want a blow-by-blow account of my movements she would want detailed notes of what I'd found out.

I read over the things I'd scribbled down while visiting the Pet Sanctuary. It didn't really amount to very much though and I was hoping that the interview with Alice would provide some clues. Firstly, I knew that Melanie was a good worker who loved animals and was interested in organizations who fought on their behalf. Filed in the back of my notebook was the folded-up leaflet from FAST that I'd picked up from Harry Smith's office. Secondly, Melanie didn't get on with the people who worked in the sanctuary. She was possessive of her own things and liable to bite people's heads off if they crossed her. Thirdly, she was friendly with Harry Smith and his wife Bernice. At least, Harry seemed genuinely to like her. I wasn't so sure about his wife, Bernice.

"We'll start, shall we?" Rosa said, pressing the button on the recorder.

Alice Tully leant against the window-sill during the interview. From time to time she looked down at the street outside. She certainly didn't seem at ease, but then I guess that was to be expected. She looked almost exactly as she had in her school photo apart from the fact that she wasn't wearing uniform. She had no make-up on that I could see but she smelled strongly of perfume.

"There are some things I need to ask you Alice, some points I want to clear up," Rosa said, perching on the edge of the table, the tape recorder nearby.

I kept my gaze on the floor. I noticed Rosa Perks' black toenails. Through her tights I could see that the varnish was chipped at the edges; not quite as perfect as the rest of her. I looked at Alice's feet. She had fragile gold sandals on, just three straps and a sole. Her toenails were ruby red, perfect and shining, as though they'd been done an hour or so before. It was a strange thing for a grieving step-sister to spend her time doing.

Was she guilty? I wondered. It was something I hadn't really considered up to that point. It wasn't part of my role to have an opinion. As well as that I really didn't know enough about the case or about Alice herself. I heard Rosa's voice.

"Tell us, in your own words, what happened the day that Melanie was poisoned."

Alice started to talk. She described the way her sister had come in from the Pet Sanctuary in a bad mood and how she had tried to be friendly by offering her some lunch. Her voice cracked a bit at this and she began to pull hard at the earring as though trying to take it off.

"Take your time, Alice," Rosa said in a soft voice.

She carried on. Most of it was stuff I already knew. Then Rosa asked her the Big Question.

"How do you think a container of arsenic with your fingerprints on it got into your bag?"

Alice pulled a tissue out of her pocket and walked up and down the room agitatedly. She looked out of the window for a few seconds. Her hair, longer now than in the photo, kept falling across her eyes and she used her fingers to comb it back. Rosa let a silence settle between the three of us. From the other office I could hear the distant sounds of chatter and the whirr of printers and fax machines. From the street below came the thin buzz of a motorbike and the honking of car horns. Alice finally spoke.

"Someone must have put it there. We all hang stuff on the hooks by the back kitchen door. Me, Mel, my dad and Sue – bags, coats. The back door's usually unlocked during the day. Whoever came in to put the poison in the food could just as easily put the container into my bag or anyone's bag for that matter."

"But how did it get your fingerprints on it?"

"I don't know. Maybe I rummaged round in my bag and touched it accidentally, when I was looking for something else."

"What, after Melanie had been poisoned, you mean?"

"I don't know! Look, if I'd intended to poison Mel would I have left the container in my own bag?"

Rosa Perks smiled at this. It was a fair point. Then she continued, "You were there all day?"

"Yes. Mel went off to the sanctuary and I had some schoolwork to do."

"Your dad and stepmum?"

"My dad was around for a while. Not that I saw him. He spends most of his time in his study downstairs. I know he went off in the afternoon to do some business. Sue was out all day, on duty at the hospital. For most of the time I was on my own."

"And did anyone call? Anybody at all? Think hard."

Alice Tully looked thoughtful. I was struck by her expression which didn't seem quite real to me; it was like an actor trying hard to show a particular emotion. Rosa didn't seem to notice.

"Wait," she said, as though it had just occurred to her, "only the milkman. He came about midday. I remember that because Sue left the money and I paid him. That was all. But then I was up in my room for most of the time, so I might not have heard."

"Why didn't you have any of the lasagne?"

"I was going to. That's why I got it out of the fridge. But I changed my mind."

"But why?"

"I don't know. I just didn't feel hungry!" Alice used her fingers to push her hair back off her face. It was beginning to irritate me and I wished that she had a couple of slides to keep it back. She seemed near to tears, and the tissue was screwed up in her other hand.

"When you decided not to eat the pasta did you put it back in the fridge or leave it out?" Rosa said.

Alice looked puzzled.

"I don't remember. Wait, I left it out, in the dish. In case I wanted it later."

"But you'd decided you didn't want it."

"That's true. At least I wasn't sure. First I thought I would, then I changed my mind."

"So you left it out in case you changed your mind again?"

"Yes. No. It wasn't as conscious as that."

"And no one else called?"

"No … no."

Alice spun the earring round several times. Her movements were jerky. Even though her expression was calm she looked agitated. I was ever so slightly suspicious of her reactions. She'd been questioned by the police for hours. She must have answered these and other questions over and over again. Why was she so uneasy? She glanced at Rosa and then at me and then back at Rosa, her eyes unable to stay on one point for very long. Was it because she felt uncomfortable putting on an act with people who were on her side?

She's lying, I thought. *Someone did call round and she doesn't want to say.*

Rosa gave the teenager a friendly smile and rubbed her hands together as if it were cold. The phone rang. She clicked off the tape recorder and pressed a button on the telephone. The receptionist's voice filled the room. *I've got Mr Tully here. He's come to pick up his daughter.*

"I'll just bring her through now," Rosa said.

Alice Tully looked mightily relieved. It was as if we were the judge and jury and we had just pronounced her innocent. She gave me a grateful smile and then followed Rosa out of the room. I wondered if she really understood how much trouble she was in. I stayed where I was and made some notes. The interview had answered a few questions, but it had left a lot more unexplained.

After a couple of minutes Rosa came back into the room. She perched on the edge of the desk and fiddled with the tape that she had just taken from the machine. Eventually she spoke. "She's holding something back."

"I agree," I said.

"I need to find out what it is before I go any further with this story. See what you can dig up on the girl."

Without another word she took the tape and went out of the room.

"Right, " I said, to no one in particular.

I scribbled a heading on my pad. DID ALICE HAVE A VISITOR?

I spent the rest of the day in the offices of NEWS TALK typing my information and thoughts on to the database. It took some time to do. A couple of the other workers stopped by the desk and had a chat, asking me why I was there and what I did for a living. One of them brought me a cup of coffee and a doughnut. It was pleasant and the time seemed to race by.

Late in the afternoon I went on to the internet. I typed in the words *animal rights* and was faced with thousands of matches. Then I typed in *Free Animals from Slavery Today*, waited for a few moments and was directed to a web page. After a few more clicks on the mouse I found myself with a plethora of information about FAST. It looked as though it was a well organized and radical group who campaigned on behalf of animals.

I downloaded a lot of the information, printed it off and took it home with me to read. A couple of the women who worked at NEWS TALK gave me a wave as I left and said, *Goodbye Patsy, see you again*.

I walked away feeling quite good. As if I was one of the crowd.

8

Door-to-Door

The next day I was sitting drinking tea at a mobile snack bar at the edge of Epping Forest. Joey Hooper was sitting opposite me and was biting into an iced bun. We'd left my car parked in Sherman Street and walked over for a break and a hot drink. It was overcast, the sky full of puffy grey clouds. Even though it wasn't cold I had my jacket on.

We'd spent the previous couple of hours doing door-to-door enquiries in Sherman Street, taking care not to be seen by the Tullys. Joey wasn't due into work until the afternoon and was helping me. We did the opposite side of the road first and then worked our way along the houses on either side of the Tullys'. We introduced ourselves as radio researchers talking about street crime. I showed my NEWS TALK badge and Joey had a pad and a pen ready to take notes.

We went from house to house. Some people weren't in; others were but were too busy to talk and told us to come back another time. A lot of people took the opportunity to have a good moan about the increase in street crime, burglaries, car theft. Nearly all of them brought up the Tully murder and spoke at length about it. Some people noticed strangers hanging round but couldn't remember anything about them; others swore to seeing odd-looking cars and people running unexpectedly.

All of them had reported their sightings to the police already and some were miffed that the police hadn't come back to tell them about developments in the case.

From my point of view, the absence of the police was one of the good things about the case. It meant that I didn't have to keep looking over my shoulder to make sure the police weren't huffing and puffing about what I was doing. Ever since I'd been working in my uncle's agency I'd made friends and enemies in the local police station. My enemies loved it when I got things wrong and were always snooty about anything I did that led to an arrest. My friends, in particular one senior female detective that I'd often worked with, were equally prickly about me stepping on their territory. *Leave the police work to the professionals*, they often said.

It was precisely because there were no police around that we were able to get on with the door-to-door without any hassle.

The neighbours were also quite chatty about the Tullys. None of the ones who actually knew the family said that they thought it was Alice who had poisoned her sister, although many of them admitted that the pair fought *like cat and dog*.

Finally we got to the immediate neighbours. The people from the house on one side had been on holiday at the time of the murder so we crossed them off the list. On the other side was the old woman who I'd spoken to the previous day. It wasn't her who answered the door though, it was her brother, whom she'd mentioned in passing. I remembered that he had been the person who had introduced Melanie to the Pet Sanctuary.

We could hear the dogs barking wildly from behind the front door. Joey nudged me and pointed to the picture of the Yorkie in the window. Just then the door opened and an old man stood in front of us. He was wearing a shirt and bow-tie covered up with a V-necked sleeveless pullover. He was at least sixty and had some of his grey hair combed across the top of his head to cover baldness.

"Mr White?" I said, smiling. "My name's Patsy Kelly and this is Joey Hooper. We're doing some investigative work on behalf of the Tully family. I had a chat with your sister yesterday about the awful business next door?" I had decided to be completely honest with the immediate neighbours.

Mr White tutted and looked next door. From behind him, somewhere in his house, I could hear his dogs yelping and scratching against wood.

"I understand that you are quite friendly with the family?"

He nodded but didn't speak.

"I wondered whether you'd seen anything unusual on the day that Melanie was killed?"

"We've already spoken to the police," he said, clearing his throat.

"We're just following it up, trying to jog people's memories."

The barking from behind was getting louder. Mr White turned and shouted something. Instead of three Yorkies it sounded more like six.

"I'm looking after a couple of dogs for a friend," Mr White explained, rolling his eyes. Then he continued talking. "Let me see, I was working in my room all day and my sister … I think my sister was baking. I think we told that to the police."

"You didn't go out at all?"

"Just to walk the dogs. My sister can't, you see, with her arthritis."

"And you didn't see any unusual cars?"

I was floundering. The old man was just shaking his head.

"I'm so busy making sure my dogs don't do their business on the pavement I hardly notice a thing," he said, cheerfully.

I walked away feeling weary, the smile on my face beginning to ache. Two hours of knocking on doors had got us a lot of background stuff but nothing that was particularly new. We decided to go for a drink up in the forest.

"How would a teenager get her hands on arsenic?" Joey said, finishing his bun.

"It's in a lot of chemical pesticides. The police haven't given out the information about which particular preparation was used."

"Rat poison?"

"It could be," I said, looking at my watch. We'd been sitting chatting for over half an hour.

"Time to go?" he said.

Leaving our cups back on the counter we started the short walk back to the car. We took a path that led through a wooded area and within minutes were away from the road and houses. After a few steps Joey put his arm around my shoulder and pulled me towards him. When he kissed me I didn't pull away.

There was something very pleasurable about kissing in broad daylight during working hours. Joey guided me backwards towards a tree as I took my glasses off and turned my head to one side. I could feel Joey's weight pushing against me as the back of my head rubbed against the bark of the tree.

After a few minutes I felt my neck going weak and decided it was time to stop.

"Hey, I'm supposed to be working!" I said, with mock anger.

"OK."

Joey pulled back. He took my glasses out of my hand and gently put them back on my face. Then he turned and walked on.

Joey was so easygoing, especially when it came to him and me. If I wanted to kiss him, fine; if I didn't there were no hurt feelings. He was keen to come out with me but never got upset if I couldn't see him or didn't feel like it. The thing about Joey was that he never put any pressure on me. He often asked me how Billy was getting on; as if nothing was happening between us. It was probably the reason that things had got this far. If Joey had wanted more from me I would have felt guilty about Billy and I would have had to make a choice.

"Did you say you went on the Net yesterday?" he said, waiting for me to catch up to him.

"Yes. I found out tons of stuff about that group I told you about. The one that Harry Smith is involved with."

"*Free Animals from Slavery Today*, wasn't it?"

"They call themselves an *information dissemination force*."

"And that is?" Joey said.

"They find out stuff about places where animals are being mistreated: laboratories, circuses, zoos, factory farming. They put it on the Net and then they produce leaflets outlining what's happening."

"And give them out. I've seen them down at the Exchange."

"Or at schools, colleges, on other demonstrations. They're trying to attract activists, people who are willing to go out and take direct action."

"Isn't that illegal?"

"It is, I know. Apparently they themselves don't actually get involved. They just give the information out, like such and such a laboratory is using monkeys for experimentation. Then other activists read it off the web or on the leaflets and they do something about it."

"Like, let them all go?"

"Yes. Or just break in and smash the equipment up. Or spray-paint slogans. All that kind of stuff."

"And Harry Smith is involved?"

"In FAST, yes. He gathers the information. Whether he gets involved in direct action or not I don't know."

We were coming to the edge of the woods. In front of us was a lane that led to Sherman Street.

"Are you actually getting anywhere with this case?" Joey said.

"I don't know. It's a puzzle. Number one, the two girls had a history of mutual dislike; number two, Alice gave the food to Melanie; number three, the container for the poison has Alice's fingerprints on it." I stopped for a minute, as though I was catching my breath, "On the other hand there's this thing called Common Sense: why on earth would Alice want to *kill* her stepsister?"

"But the police think she did it?"

"So it seems. I keep thinking they must know something that we don't."

If there was a downside to the absence of the police

then this was it. It was one thing not having them moaning at me, but it was quite another not knowing the full details of the case. Rosa had a contact, that was true; but how much was he passing on to her? And how much of that was she passing on to me?

Joey was quiet for a moment. I was thinking aloud. "Family and friends. That's where you usually start with a murder. The trouble is that I've got no access to Melanie's family and Alice seems to be the obvious suspect. I don't even know if Rosa believes that she's innocent. She just wants a good programme."

I could see the corner of Sherman Street coming up and I began to rummage in my rucksack for my car keys. Just then I noticed an old blue van parked further up with two people sitting in it talking. Screwing my eyes up I could make out some kind of sticker on the back door. It looked familiar.

"Wait," I said, not wanting to get too near.

I was close enough to see the letters on the sticker: FAST.

The passenger door opened suddenly and a young woman got out. She was tall, with long hair, and I'd spent time with her the previous day.

"Alice Tully, " I said.

I pulled Joey behind a car and made him stand back. Alice Tully was bent over shouting something into the van. I couldn't hear her words but the tone was one of anger. She was half leaning into the van, speaking rapidly. Then she stood up straight and slammed the door.

I waited a moment before I stepped out and watched her disappear around the corner into Sherman Street. The blue van pulled carelessly away from the pavement and began a jerky three-point turn. I pulled Joey back behind the car and waited until the van had turned itself round and was facing us.

Harry Smith was sitting behind the wheel. He glanced behind him at the corner of Sherman Street. Then he shook his head and drove off.

I stood up straight.

"Alice Tully and Harry Smith," I said. "How do they know each other?"

"Perhaps they met. You know, like When Harry Met Alice!"

I wasn't listening. There had been nothing in any of the notes about *Alice* Tully being involved with the Pet Sanctuary. How was it that she knew Harry Smith? Had she met him through Melanie? Joey was still talking.

"See it's like *When Harry Met Sally*. Get it? When Harry Met Alice."

I gave him what I hoped was a withering look.

"Why didn't Alice mention knowing Harry Smith?" I said it out loud but it was just one of a lot of questions that I was asking in my head.

"Did you ask her?" Joey said.

"Well, no," I said

It was Joey's turn to give me a look, and I duly withered.

9

The Past

My dad had cooked a vegetarian lasagne and he took it out of the oven with a flourish.

"There!" he said. "Completely organic."

He was wearing a pair of blue and white striped oven gloves. He placed the dish on a mat in the centre of the table. The cheese on the top was still bubbling. Me, my mum and Gerry were sitting around Billy's kitchen table waiting for him to cut into it.

"Since when have you been a vegetarian?" my mum said.

"I saw this TV programme about factory farming a while back. Animals cooped up in tiny pens, pumped full of antibiotics. I've not eaten meat since."

"What about fish?"

It was the first thing Gerry had said since we'd

arrived. I was surprised at how quiet he was; he usually had an opinion to offer on almost any subject. He looked different as well. He was still wearing his jeans but he'd put a proper shirt and tie on and from the waist up looked almost respectable.

"It's like this, Gerry, it's not that I'm against eating the flesh of animals. It's just that I don't approve of the way they are farmed and slaughtered."

The word *slaughter* made me flinch.

"We've all got this cosy picture of farming. When I was a kid, farms were small places with a few cows and pigs and hens laying eggs just outside the kitchen door. Eating meat then, it seemed the most healthy thing in the world."

"You don't know what you're eating, nowadays," my mum said, "that's why I buy free-range eggs. They're more expensive though," she added, with a sigh.

Gerry looked like he was going to say something but he didn't. He had no problems eating meat, I knew that. Every time my mum got him to go to the supermarket he came back with a joint of beef and packets of pork chops.

My dad finished ladling the food out and there was quiet for a minute while we tucked in.

"Mmm…" my mum made a noise and gave my dad a warm smile.

Gerry looked up at that moment and saw my parents smiling at each other. He bent his head down, took a mouthful of food and concentrated on chewing it. He was feeling uncomfortable, I knew. Since my dad had showed up Gerry had lost some of his confidence.

The previous evening he'd come into the living room carrying a cup of tea and a plate of chocolate biscuits.

I'd been pondering over Alice Tully and Harry Smith, and how they might have met. It had to be through Melanie, I'd decided. What I hadn't been able to work out was why it hadn't been mentioned by anyone.

"Made this for you, Pats," Gerry said, handing me the unexpected snack.

I pulled myself out of my thoughts and took the tea. I'd given up asking him not to shorten my name to *Pats*. Actually, I'd got used to it. He sat beside me on the sofa and rubbed his hands together as though he were about to undertake some physical task.

"It's nice for you that your dad's around," he said, lacing his fingers in and out of each other.

"Yes," I said.

Truthfully, it hadn't really made much difference to my life. It wasn't like he was a long-lost father whom I desperately missed while he'd lived in Birmingham. It was nice to know I was going to see him a bit over the next few weeks, but on the other hand I wasn't unhappy that he was moving to Crete. My dad and me simply weren't that close.

"What happened when your mum and dad split

up?" Gerry said it quietly, as though there was no real urgency in the question.

"I was only five."

"But your mum's told you some stuff about it."

"Hasn't she told you?" I said, surprised.

"Bits and pieces…"

"Why don't you ask her?" I said. It wasn't like Gerry to hang back if there was something he wanted to know.

"It's not really my business…"

He looked sheepish, like a kid who wanted something but couldn't actually get the words out to ask for it. I felt sorry for him. "My mum and dad's marriage was never very good, that's what she told me."

"Really?" Gerry tried to look sympathetic.

"They weren't exactly suited, she being a teacher and him a salesman. He was always off after this and that deal. He worked on commission and it was all about weekly and monthly targets."

I paused. The information came out like a story, but it had taken years for my mum to tell it to me, piece by piece, until it made a whole. Gerry was looking hard at me, waiting for the next bit. It occurred to me then that Gerry and my mum weren't particularly well matched either.

"A couple of years after I was born my mum got a job in a local college. She was delighted. She had a husband who she cared for, a daughter and a perfect job which was just down the road from where she lived. A few months later, my dad was offered a job based in Liverpool. He wanted us all to move."

I shrugged my shoulders. Gerry was rapt with attention.

"My mum refused. They came to an arrangement. He took a cheap flat up in Liverpool and lived up there Monday to Friday. At weekends he came home. That went on for about nine months."

I drank my tea. I was telling the story in a matter of fact way. It was as though I wasn't talking about my own family at all, just some people that I knew.

"One January there was this big storm, and it blew a lot of the tiles off the college roof. The rain got into the electrics and shorted out the central heating. The college was shut for a week and the staff were told to work at home. I was about four, I think. My mum made a spur of the moment decision to go up to Liverpool and surprise my dad."

"That was when she found him with someone else?" Gerry said.

I looked at him for a moment. He had a sheepish expression on his face. It hadn't been so long before that I had caught *him* in the arms of another woman. It hadn't been serious, he'd said and begged me not to tell my mum. I hadn't, and I'd often wondered whether I'd done the right thing. I forced my mind back to the story my mum had told me about the trip to Liverpool.

"It was much worse than that," I said.

"Go on," Gerry said.

"Me and my mum went up on the train. I was so excited."

I didn't remember any of this. It was all part of the fragmented story my mum had told me. *You were so excited*, she'd said, *being on a real train*.

"We went round to his flat. My mum had been there a couple of times to visit him so she knew where it was. But he wasn't there. I mean he wasn't *living* there any more. A man gave us a forwarding address. He'd been sending my dad's mail on for three months."

"He hadn't told your mum he'd moved?"

"No. He'd told my mum that the landlord had disconnected the phone and he could only be contacted through work. He usually rang her from phone boxes."

There was a vague feeling of annoyance stirring inside me. I'd known this story for many years, even discussed it with my mum on occasions. I'd never told it quite like this though. I'd never put it in order and described each bit so clearly. It was as if it was being played out again in front of me.

"We went round to the new address, knocked on the door. It was opened by a blonde woman. My mum said she was very pretty and as thin as a pipe-cleaner. She was pleasant and nice. She must have gone inside and spoken to my dad because he came out a few seconds later. My mum said he looked like he'd seen a ghost."

"He was staying with this woman?"

"He was *living* with her. He had been for three months. She had no idea he was married with a kid."

"But what about going home at weekends?"

"He told this woman that his mother was old and housebound and that he liked to spend part of every weekend with her. She believed him. Just like my mum believed that he was on his own for five days every week."

Gerry sat back on the sofa, his face a picture of amazement.

"She never told me. Not all of it." He said it with a kind of wonder; as if the story had been juicier than he'd thought. Then he absentmindedly reached over to the plate of chocolate biscuits and took a couple.

After we'd eaten the food my dad cleared the plates away. Then he brought out a trifle that he'd made, which was heavily laced with brandy; the smell of it was making my eyes water.

"Mmm," my mum said and held her bowl out for the trifle. As my dad scooped some out of the dish he seemed to keep his eyes on her as if studying her face. Gerry noticed it too and took a large gulp of his drink.

The next morning I had breakfast with my mum. The radio was playing quietly in the background and the smell of toast filled the room. I had my case file on the table. Gerry was still in bed.

"It's nice for you to see a bit more of your dad," my mum said.

She was reading the newspaper, her glasses pushed up on to the top of her head. On the plate was a piece of toast that she'd cut into triangles.

"Is Gerry all right?" I said.

"He didn't have that much to drink."

"No, I mean is he all right about my dad being here?"

"Why shouldn't he be?" My mum put the newspaper down and put her glasses on to give me a look of puzzlement.

"I don't know," I said. "I just wondered."

I heard the phone ringing and went out to the hall, a piece of toast still in my hand.

"Patsy? It's Rosa," a voice said, as soon as I answered.

"Yes?"

"Something's happened. I need you to meet me at the Tullys' place."

"What is it?" I said.

"I think Alice Tully's done a bunk. Her parents have been on to me. They're in a bit of a state. Can you meet me there in, say, half an hour?"

"Fine. I'm—"

I was about to say that I was dressed and ready to go but Rosa had ended the call. I replaced the receiver, my thoughts racing ahead of me. Alice Tully gone. What did it mean? I looked up the stairs to see Gerry coming down. He was wearing jogging bottoms and a T-shirt. His hair was standing up at the front and he was yawning. I gave him an absentminded smile and went into the kitchen to pick up my stuff. My mum was standing up, getting her things together. She was smartly dressed and in her hand she had a sleek leather briefcase with a name tag that said *Ms Kelly, English Department*. Gerry pushed the door open.

"Aren't you going into college for a lecture?" my mum said sharply.

"I've got time for a coffee," Gerry said, sleepily.

"Not if you want a lift from me," my mum said, pushing past him and walking out into the hall. I followed her out.

"I'll get the bus."

"Suit yourself."

My mum opened the front door and I followed her out.

"Where are you off to?" she said, one eye looking past me at the house.

"Developments in the case," I said. "It looks like this Alice Tully has—"

"Good. That's nice," my mum said, opening her car door and getting in.

I watched her drive off and looked back at the house where Gerry was probably sitting alone in the kitchen hugging a cup of coffee. Since my dad had come back things were different. It was lucky that I was too busy to think about it.

10

Missing

Sue Tully opened the front door. Behind her was Rosa Perks.

"Hi," I said, in a friendly but hushed voice.

I wasn't quite sure how to act. Rosa beckoned me to follow her into the living room and I sat myself down quickly on an armchair. When I looked up I could see that the room was full of vases of flowers and sympathy cards. Sue Tully had sat herself on the very edge of the sofa, her legs together, her hands clasping her knees. She was thin with brown jaw-length hair and a fringe that had been cut too short. Her face was colourless, her skin lifeless and yellow-looking. All the time she seemed to be grinding her back teeth. Even though she wasn't making a noise it set my nerves on edge.

Rosa was standing by the fireplace in her usual

black and white. She looked at me and pretended to write on her hand. It was a signal for me to get my pad out. Yet again I was to be the silent secretary figure. I sighed.

Frank Tully came in. He glanced at me for a second but then his eyes flicked away. He either hadn't remembered seeing me or it had become unimportant to him.

"Mr Tully, this is my associate, Miss Kelly. She's been assisting me in this investigation. Perhaps you'd be kind enough to describe the events again."

Frank Tully looked momentarily annoyed, as if he had done enough explaining. He seemed to notice his wife then and went across and sat next to her. He put his hand on her arm and she seemed to stiffen and shift further into the corner of the seat. If he noticed he didn't show it.

"It was just before midnight last night. Sue and I were in here and Alice was upstairs. She'd been in all evening. That's part of her bail conditions you see, she's not allowed out after eight. Not that she's wanted to go anywhere."

He stopped. I wasn't sure if he was upset or just plain angry. His wife seemed completely still, her hands gripped together like a vice.

"I heard her footsteps down the stairs and then the front door opened. At first we thought that someone had come. Even though it was late I thought that it might have been the police. When no one came in I went out there. I left Sue in here, didn't I love? I went out into the hall and found the front door wide open."

"And she was gone?" Rosa said, gently.

"She was out, on the street, standing in front of this blue van. I shouted out for her to come back in. She knew she wasn't allowed out at night."

Sue Tully spoke, her words like little icicles, "It was her boyfriend."

"No, we don't know that. We don't even know that she's got a boyfriend."

Rosa gave me a knowing look. I'd told her about seeing Alice Tully in Harry Smith's van the day before.

"I came in. I thought she'd followed me. Then I heard doors slamming and a car moving off. I went over to the window. Sue was there, weren't you love? I thought she'd come back in. I gave it a couple of minutes then I went out. She was gone. I walked up and down the street but there was no sign of her."

"And you think she's run away."

"I don't know."

"Have you told the police?" I said, forgetting that I wasn't supposed to speak.

"No, I can't do that," he said.

"Of course he can't," Rosa said, a touch of exasperation in her voice. "Alice has been under a tremendous amount of stress. If she has gone off somewhere and broken her bail conditions, then it could look very bad for her. When did she last report in to the police station?"

"Yesterday morning. I took her in the car," Frank Tully said.

"She's run away," Sue Tully said, her words heavy and uncompromising.

Frank Tully took his hand off his wife's arm. He coughed a couple of times and then used his fingers to comb back his grey hair. I was reminded of Alice doing the same thing.

"I'll make some tea," he said and stood up.

"I'll help you," Rosa said, brightly.

They left Sue Tully sitting like a statue on the end of the settee, and I could hear cups rattling in the distance. A thin grey cat appeared suddenly from behind a chair. Its coat was short and shiny. It walked hesitantly across the carpet and then leant sideways against Sue Tully's legs. It was as thin as bootlaces, its face skeletal. It let out a purr that seemed to vibrate through the quiet room. I didn't speak for a minute. I was supposed to keep quiet, I knew, but Sue Tully seemed to want to talk.

"Melanie loved this cat," she said, "Alice hates it."

"I can't believe you think that Alice…"

I was going to say *killed* Melanie but I couldn't get the word out. It didn't matter. Sue Tully knew exactly what I was getting at.

"He doesn't think so. But then he wouldn't."

"You say she had a boyfriend?"

"I've seen her talking to this lad in a blue van. The same one for weeks now. He was Melanie's friend from the sanctuary. I heard the two girls arguing over him."

I wasn't writing anything, just letting Sue Tully pour out her anger. I didn't want to tell her that Harry Smith was married.

"You think Alice killed her sister over a boyfriend?"

"They weren't real sisters. They lived in the same house, but there wasn't much between them. They could barely stand being in the same room together."

"But to poison—"

"All I know is my daughter was alive when I went to work, and when I came home she was dead, and Alice's fingerprints are on the bottle that held the poison." Her voice had lowered to a whisper. "Melanie's dead and all Alice can do is spray perfume on and run out of the house to meet that boy in the van. I've been watching her, collecting evidence. Last night, when she went out I even took the number of the van. I was looking through this window, see, and I memorized most of the number. Here, I wrote it down."

She took a piece of paper out of her pocket and held it in front of my face. On it was part of a registration number: T421 B. Beside it was the word *Ford*.

"She did it. Alice killed my Melanie. I know it. It's the only reason that I'm staying here. I want to keep an eye on her."

She pushed the paper into my hand, nodding her head all the while.

The living-room door opened and Rosa came in with Frank Tully. I put the piece of paper in my pocket and sat back down. Sue Tully perched on the edge of the settee like a wounded bird. From time to time she looked meaningfully at me. I just sipped at my tea. After about fifteen minutes we got up to go. Rosa said she'd keep in touch with the Tullys and made a lot of sympathetic noises. As we were walking away down the path I heard the dogs barking from next door.

"What a racket," Rosa said. "If I lived next door to that I'd complain!"

"They're only Yorkshire Terriers," I said.

"All the same…"

Rosa stood by my car and I assumed she wanted a lift. Once inside she pulled out her mobile phone and began poking at its buttons. All the while she hadn't said anything. With a sigh she put the phone back into her bag.

"I think this case is going nowhere."

"I disagree."

I said it with a tiny bit of excitement in my voice. I then proceeded to tell her about Sue Tully's comments and the fact that she had taken some of the registration of the van that Alice disappeared into.

"What if she has done a bunk? What if she did poison her sister?" Rosa said, gloomily. "That means the programme's definitely off."

"What if she hasn't?" I said. "What if someone's taken her?"

I don't really know why I said it. I didn't believe it, not then. I honestly thought she'd gone off somewhere with Harry Smith. Whether she'd killed her sister or not I wasn't sure. All I knew was that I was intrigued. I wanted to get to the bottom of it.

"She could have been kidnapped!" I said, trying to raise Rosa's interest.

Rosa sat up as though someone had just injected her with something.

"You could be right! Think about it. Her parents think she's broken her bail conditions so they don't go to the police when really, all the time, she's been taken away by someone. Perhaps the real murderer."

Rosa went on in this vein. By the time we'd reached the NEWS TALK offices she had mapped out the whole thing and it sounded like it was her idea in the first place. A kidnap of an innocent victim by a murderer in order to cover up his or her tracks.

"What a scoop it would be!" she said, with wonder in her voice.

That was what it boiled down to. A great news story. A chance for Rosa Perks to stun the world of journalism by rescuing the girl from a kidnapper and proving her innocent at the same time.

"Give me this afternoon to reach my contacts. I'll sort out this registration number and then we can move on from there. I'll ring you tonight."

And then she was gone, her high heels bouncing up the stairs and into the NEWS TALK offices. I knew she didn't care about the case, but it didn't matter. She had the contacts to find out about the vehicle registration number. I was still ninety-eight per cent convinced that it was Harry Smith.

In the afternoon I went to see Joey Hooper. I found him in the frozen food section of the supermarket where he worked.

"I'm on my break in about ten minutes. Can you hang around till then? I've got some interesting news," he said, tidying up bags of frozen chips.

"So have I," I said.

I went and bought a tea and a tuna mayonnaise roll and sat in the supermarket cafeteria. I wasn't really thinking about what Joey had just said. I was thinking about Alice Tully and Harry Smith. How had they met? Were they in a relationship? Had Melanie been jealous? Could it have been a reason why there was further animosity between the sisters?

I sat and watched as people paid the cashier and carried their trays carefully along, looking from side to side to see if there was a vacant table. Sitting down, they unloaded their meal and drink and then looked quizzically for a place to put the tray. Most of them ended up filing it on the floor between the chairs. Then they would pick up their knife and fork and start to eat.

Alice Tully said she had heated up the food for her sister. It seemed an odd thing for her to do when the girls didn't get on. I thought back to the poison.

Arsenic. I'd looked it up on the internet when I'd been in the NEWS TALK offices the previous day. It was a natural substance, an element. It was in the world around us, in the soil and the water. It was in our food chain and we were all taking some of it into our systems every day. It had no taste or smell and in small amounts it didn't necessarily kill a person. In large amounts it was fatal. I'd read that it was used widely in the nineteenth- and early twentieth-centuries in various household goods. It had also been used in several celebrated cases where wives had attempted to do away with husbands, or vice versa. Often they administered the poison in small amounts for weeks. The victim suffered diarrhoea and vomiting so it looked as though they'd died of some natural cause. Before the days of sophisticated forensic investigations a killer could literally get away with murder.

Nowadays that simply wasn't possible. Post-mortems detected the most minute traces of any drug in a victim's system. Alice Tully was a bright girl and she would have known this. If she had wanted to kill her sister, surely she would have done it some other way?

I saw Joey coming towards me from the far side of the restaurant. I gave a little wave.

"Hey, how are you?" Joey said, sitting down opposite me.

"Good. There've been some developments."

I told him what had happened that morning. He

sat with his hands loosely clasped, and a noticeable frown on his forehead. It was a forced expression rather than one of real interest. He was keen to change the subject, I thought.

"What's your news?" I said, drinking the rest of my tea.

His face brightened up and he reached out and grabbed my hand.

"Some friends of my mum and dad in Brighton are having a party. They weren't going to bother going, but now they've changed their minds. They're going to be away on Saturday night. The house is empty. I thought you could stay over."

It took a minute for it to sink in. Joey wanted me to *stay over*. He wanted me to spend the night at his house when his mum and dad weren't there.

"Don't look so pleased about it," he said, genuinely puzzled this time. I felt his hand a little looser in mine.

"No! It sounds great. Only I can't."

"Why not?" he said, pulling back to his side of the table.

I didn't have a good reason. I didn't have anywhere else to go. I was old enough to sleep away from home without asking my mum's permission. There was no excuse. It was just that the idea of it filled me with guilt.

"I thought we could go out somewhere then bring a take-away back to my place. We'd be all on our *own*."

I knew what he was getting at. I just didn't know if I was ready for it.

"Thing is…" I said, unsure as to how to finish the sentence. I didn't need to. A look of irritation settled on his face.

"Patsy, what is it with you? You spend all your time coming on strong to me. You're all over me when we're together. Now we got a chance to spend some time alone and you're not interested?"

"It's just that Billy—"

There. I'd mentioned his name. How could I spend the night with Joey when Billy and I were still a couple? On my bedside table there was a letter from Billy that I'd received not two weeks before. Somewhere in that letter were the words *I do still love you*.

"If you're so worried about Billy how come we're spending time together at all?"

"We're friends…" I started, knowing as I spoke that it was a weak argument.

"I've got a lot of friends, Patsy, and I don't do the things with them that I do with you; know what I'm saying?"

I did know what he was saying. I looked down into my cup. The bottom of it was empty. No tea leaves there for me to look into the future.

"Face up to it, you're not bothered about me. I'm just someone to play around with while your real boyfriend's away."

"That's just not true." I said.

I didn't know whether it was true or not. All I knew was that spending the night with Joey was like making a statement. *We are a couple*. Then I couldn't go on writing chatty letters to Billy.

He stood up suddenly and the table rattled where it hit his leg.

"Goodbye, Patsy," he said, his voice dull and emotionless.

I could have walked after him. I could have remonstrated with him, argued with him, tried to persuade him to give me a bit more time. I didn't though. I watched him get further away and felt a flurry of frustration inside my chest. My trouble was I wanted it all. A boyfriend in Africa and Joey here in London.

That evening I got a phone call from Rosa.

"Hi Patsy," she said, "I've just spoken to my police contact."

"Did you find out anything?"

"As you know we only had a bit of the registration number. That's why it took so long. He had to put the numbers into the national computer. Needless to say I didn't tell him what it was for."

"There must be thousands of blue Ford vans."

"That's true. But not all with those letters in their registration and not all in this area. We've narrowed it down to twelve. And here's the interesting bit. One of them belongs to Wendy Smith, proprietor of the Pet Sanctuary in Loughton."

Sue Tully had been right. So much for the kidnap theory.

"I got one of the girls in the office to do a quick ring round. All the vans were accounted for at the time Alice went missing except for two. The Pet Sanctuary van and one from a hire company in Stratford. In the morning I want you to go up to Loughton and sniff around. If Alice went with Harry then she has some explaining to do. I have a feeling that there's more to it than meets the eye. You may as well go down to the hire company too. It's called VANLOAN and it's on the Riverway Industrial Park. Check it out, find out who hired the van, etcetera, etcetera. No point in leaving loose ends."

"What about the Tullys. Will you tell them?"

"No. I'll wait till we've got something more concrete. If this Harry Smith is involved it could open up the investigation."

Before I could answer her the call ended abruptly. I was left with unspoken thoughts. Didn't Rosa have any social graces? Would it cost a lot for her to say "Goodbye, Patsy?"

Goodbye, Patsy. I remembered the phrase from earlier in the day.

I went to bed thinking about Joey and Billy and Alice and Harry. After a while I fell into a fitful sleep.

11

Searching

I woke up with an emotional hangover, still feeling bad about Joey Hooper. I forced it out of my mind, glad that I had concrete things to do, visits to make, people to see. All the same, I paused before starting my car up and held my mobile phone in my hand. A quick call could make everything all right. On the other hand it could make matters worse. I zipped my phone up in my bag and drove off.

For some reason I went to the van-hire place at Stratford first. Maybe it was because I wanted to get it out of the way before I took the long drive to Loughton. Maybe it was because I wasn't sure how to approach Harry Smith, and what to do if he simply denied any knowledge of Alice's whereabouts.

I looked it up in the A–Z and after some difficult navigation down by the river I found the company garages tucked in the far corner of the small industrial estate. VANLOAN. *You want a van? We've got it!* a cheerful sign said. I parked the car in a yard beside three blue vans and a much older cream one. A young lad was hoovering out the inside of the one on the end. The next van was the one I had down on my list, T421 BMH.

The office was in a small Portakabin. I went inside and waited while a grey-haired man finished off his conversation with a middle-aged blonde woman who was sitting in an armchair behind a desk. In front of her was an electric typewriter, something I hadn't seen for a long time. They were talking about weddings. I sighed to myself.

"Aubergine satin. I ask you! In the middle of winter. Would you wear aubergine?"

"Aubergine? What colour's that?" the man said, as though it was something that he might consider.

I'd already worked out something to say. I looked at my watch. It shouldn't take long. All I had to do was to get the name and address of the person who hired the van, go and see them and find out where it was when Alice Tully was abducted. It was just a case of eliminating it before I went to the Pet Sanctuary.

"What can I do for you, darlin'?" The woman said, when the man finally made an exit.

"Hi," I said, in a friendly way. "I wonder if you can help me. There was an accident in my street the other night and someone driving one of your vans was a witness."

"Yes?"

The woman was rolling a piece of paper into the typewriter. The armchair she was sitting on looked incongruous against the flat walls of the Portakabin. I noticed, on the side of the desk, a china plate with custard creams on it and a matching china cup and saucer.

"I wrote down his van number and the name of your company. I thought I wrote the guy's name down but I've looked everywhere and I can't find it," I said.

"Our van wasn't involved though?"

"No, not at all. Like I said. The driver was a witness."

"Which van was it? You can see we've got a few." She let out a loud laugh at this, and I smiled and read the registration number out.

"The T-reg? Let me see…"

She took out a book from a drawer and flicked back a few pages. I wondered why news of the computer revolution hadn't reached this sleepy little company. My eyes wandered to the other side of the desk where there was a pile of magazines: *Brides and Setting Up Home*, *Weddings* and *First Homes*.

"Here we are. A Mr Raymond, 17 Dorset Street, E17. Insurance through Crown Brokers."

Feeling really pleased with myself I scribbled it down. It hadn't taken more than five minutes and the woman had been so helpful. I found myself getting chatty.

"My mum got married a couple of months ago. It wasn't a white wedding. She wore a cream dress and jacket. She looked really nice."

"Very tasteful. I'm wearing midnight-blue velvet myself. Winter wedding, you see."

"And your daughter?" I said, remembering the aubergine satin. It certainly would clash with the midnight-blue velvet.

She laughed.

"It's me who's getting married, dear. My daughter's been married for ten years."

I left the office apologizing and feeling silly. I heard her laughing to herself as I closed the door behind me.

In the car I looked up the A-Z. I had to hold the index pages far away in order to focus on the tiny print. I scanned up and down but I couldn't find Dorset St, E17. Puzzled, I looked again following the line of street names down with my finger. Perhaps it had been E15 or N17. There was a Dorset Avenue in SE17 but I was sure it couldn't be that.

In the end I had to accept that there was no Dorset Street in E17. I was stumped. I held my scribbled notes up. The car insurance was through Crown Brokers. Maybe they would have the correct address. I rang directory enquiries on my mobile and gave the name of the company. I said it was probably in East London. A disembodied voice read out a number and I wrote it down carefully.

A man answered almost as soon as it started to ring.

"Crown Brokers. How may I help?" he said and cleared his throat a couple of times. His words were polite but his voice sounded bored.

"I'm ringing from VANLOAN," I said, "One of our customers has his insurance through you. I'm just doing a security check on his address." I was speaking as though I'd learned a script, natural and easy.

"We don't give out information on our clients," the man said, the tone of his voice flat. Now that he realized I wasn't a potential customer he could afford to show his true mood. He continued to cough on the other end of the line. I was willing to bet that he had a cigarette on the end of his fingers.

"I don't want any information," I lied, trying to keep him sweet, "I just wondered if you'd confirm his address. It's a Mr Raymond of 17 Dorset Street, E17."

There was a moment of silence from the other end, as if the man was deciding whether to cut me off or not. I couldn't stand the suspense.

"It's a new system. We make random checks on the information we're given. I'm sure you're in exactly the same boat as we are."

The man gave an earsplitting cough. Then he spoke.

"We have no one of that name on our records. I'm afraid someone has given you false information."

"I see," I said. "Thank you very much. You've been a great help."

I ended the call and sat very still in the car. The person who had hired the van had given a false name and details. It didn't necessarily mean that they had been responsible for Alice Tully's supposed abduction but it was strange all the same. I was about to ring Rosa and tell her when I noticed that the young man who had been cleaning the vans was walking towards the Portakabin.

I made a snap decision. I got out of the car and walked quickly towards the vans. I could see, through the glass of the Portakabin, the young man talking to the woman. They both had their backs to where the vans were parked. The back of the T-reg van was unlocked so I opened the doors and leaned in. It was empty, of course. It was also quite mucky as though someone had been moving a load of garden rubbish in it. I closed the doors and went round to the front. The passenger side was unlocked as well so I got in. I looked around the floor and down the pockets of each door.

I didn't really know what I was looking for. The van was empty as far as I could see. Then I pulled down the glove compartment.

A parking ticket fell out. It was in a plastic envelope and looked as though it had been screwed up before being shoved in the glove compartment. I flattened it out and read it over. The van had been illegally parked on a disabled parking bay the previous day at High Street, Abbeyfield, Essex. The time was 9.16 am.

I sat back for a minute. If the customer used the van out in Essex it probably meant that it wasn't near Leytonstone the night before. Maybe the person had no insurance and that was why they gave a false address? It wasn't conclusive either way. I looked at my watch. It was almost eleven o'clock. I tucked the parking ticket into my bag and decided to leave it for Rosa to sort out. It was time to head off up to Loughton.

I pulled down the passenger mirror and had a look at my face. Don't ask me why. Maybe it was just a girly thing to do. I licked my finger and smoothed out my eyebrows. My glasses looked smeared but I didn't have the energy to clean them. I glanced over at the Portakabin and saw that the boy was sitting down with a mug of something in his hand.

In the mirror my skin was looking tired. I could do with a facial, a long bath, some hair conditioner and an early night. On the other hand, I could see Joey Hooper and sort out the problems between us. My skin and hair would perk up then. Feeling depressed, I knew, was murder on your appearance. I was about to flip the mirror up when a gleam of something caught my eye from behind. I looked round into the back of the van. The sun was shining through the door windows and something was glittering on the floor.

I got out, walked round the back and pulled open the back door. From where I was standing it was hard to see anything. The interior of the van was pitch black. I screwed up my eyes and leaned in, letting my fingers feel across the dusty surface.

After a few moments I felt it there. Small and round. I stepped back and looked at it in the light. It was a gold hoop earring. Just like the one that Alice Tully had worn during her interview at NEWS TALK. She'd been nervous, I remembered, and had kept fiddling with it.

I held it tightly in my hand. I was pushing down a feeling of excitement. It was a common enough earring. Someone loading garden rubbish might have snagged it on some branches without knowing. It could happen.

But for two things. Firstly, whoever had hired the van had lied about their address and insurance and probably their name as well. Secondly, a blue Ford van with a similar – if not identical – registration plate had been involved when the girl disappeared. It was too much of a coincidence. There was only one conclusion I could draw.

Alice Tully had been in the back of that van.

12

Abbeyfield

I drove straight to Abbeyfield in Essex. It wasn't as far as it sounded, about twenty minutes beyond Epping. Being a Londoner, anywhere outside the tube network was deep countryside to me. Abbeyfield was no exception.

I'd rung Rosa Perks and had to leave a very long message on her voice mail. I told her all about the van and urged her to contact the police. *Never mind the news story*, I'd said. *The most important thing is to try and find Alice*. I was beginning to feel jittery about the absence of the police. In the past I'd always been able to get hold of someone involved in a case if I got into deep water. This time I was once removed from anyone with authority. The very first case I'd ever investigated had involved a supposedly kidnapped girl who had turned up dead because we hadn't got to her in time. I had had bad feelings about it for a long time afterwards and I didn't want a repetition.

As soon as I left the dual carriageway I plunged into winding lanes and dipped in and out of fields and woods until I eventually got to Abbeyfield.

It was a small village. The main square was about the size of a football field and in the middle was a duck pond. It looked like a picture postcard. Around the green was a small supermarket, a pub and a couple of antique shops. There didn't seem to be anyone about.

I drove up and parked along from the supermarket. Just in front there was a yellow disabled parking bay. It must have been where the van was parked the morning after Alice Tully went missing. I looked around at the shops and wondered if anyone would remember it. There was hardly anyone to ask. I frowned to myself. Even though I'd driven here I wasn't exactly sure what I could find out. I imagined myself walking along the road, knocking on doors asking if anyone remembered seeing the van. And in the unlikely event that someone had seen it what could they tell me? It was a blue Ford hire van. There was every likelihood that it was just passing through. Possibly the driver stopped to go into the supermarket and buy some food or cigarettes.

I had an idea. I turned the ignition and moved my car forward for ten metres or so until it was parked firmly in the disabled bay. People might not remember a blue van, but they might remember someone who was illegally parked in a place reserved for people with disabilities.

I got out of the car and went into the supermarket. It was a long narrow shop with two aisles. All the time I walked up one and down the other I kept an eye on my car outside. I spent about five minutes looking at magazines. Then I picked up a chicken salad sandwich and a small bottle of water and walked towards the till. An older woman in half-moon glasses looked at me with some hostility. Whether it was because I was young and an outsider or because my car was illegally parked I wasn't sure. I kept quiet, hoping that she would build up a head of steam. I put my money down as she peered over the top of her glasses for the prices of my items. I didn't show any signs of impatience, I just let her take her time. After ringing each amount up she looked hard at me. I smiled sweetly back. How long would it take for her to overcome her reserve and tell me off about parking my car there, I wondered?

A woman with a small child came up behind me and I moved so that she could put her wire basket down. She exchanged a greeting with the shopkeeper who smiled at her and turned to me to take my money. As she gave me my change she cleared her throat.

"I hope you don't mind me saying but you really should avoid parking there," she said pointing out of the window, her finger long and thin, her hand trembling slightly.

"Oh, really?" I said.

"It's for disabled drivers."

"Oh, I'm sorry. Trust me not to read the road signs. I'm not from round here, you see."

"They're not all that clear," the mother behind me said.

"Are you from the holiday cottages?" the shop-keeper asked.

"Yes," I lied.

"I really must tell the owner to inform his clients of the local by-laws. You can get a fine. Only a couple of days ago a man parked on the edge of it. His van was only about a metre into the bay but a passing police car put a ticket on it. He was very upset, I can tell you."

"He was upset," the mother said, "I saw him screwing the ticket into a ball."

"Was he from the holiday cottages?" I said, in a chatty way.

"No, I don't think so."

"No, he wasn't," the woman behind me said. "I saw the van go past my cottage down Friar Lane. He could be staying at Birch Farm. That's the only place down that way that's habitable."

I wanted to ask about the man. Was he young or old? Tall or short? What did he look like? How did he speak? Instead I picked up my purchases and walked off back to my car. All the while I was thinking *Friar Lane, Birch Farm, Friar Lane, Birch Farm*. When I got into my seat I wrote it down.

I rang Rosa again but she wasn't there. I left another long message urging her to get moving. Then I drove off through the village until I reached a tiny garage at the end. I got out, bought some petrol and then asked the attendant about Friar Lane. The man, dressed from head to foot in spotless green overalls, gave me explicit and over-long directions. He looked like he was glad to have someone to talk to. I asked him about Birch Farm.

"Used to be one of those kennel places. Where people put their dogs when they went on holiday. I didn't know it was a holiday…"

"Thanks," I said, backing away from him and getting into the car. I gave him a wave as I set off in the direction of Friar Lane.

It was a narrow lane which was wide enough for one car. Every hundred metres or so there was a passing place in case I met any other vehicle coming head on. I didn't pass anything. I went by some cottages near the start but after that there were only fields and hedges. About halfway down there were some empty houses, a row of six in all, their windows boarded up, looking rundown and battered by the elements. A couple had parts of their roofs missing. A sign next to them said, *ABBEYFIELD REDEVELOPMENT: Providing homes for all*. The lane turned into a dirt track not long after that and I made my way along it with great care. The last thing I wanted was a puncture while I was out in the middle of nowhere.

In the distance I could see what looked like some farm buildings. I slowed down and stopped the car by some bushes. There didn't seem to be anyone about; no people, no dogs, no livestock. Just up ahead I saw a battered sign that looked like it had seen better days: *Birch Farm and Kennels, Proprietors Mr and Mrs Watt*.

I closed the car and picked up my bag. Maybe this place had nothing to do with anything; the man in the blue van could have been simply passing through here or have taken a wrong turning. I walked ahead, shouting out, "Hello, is anyone there?" If someone was at home I could say I was lost, and ask to use the phone or the toilet.

I knocked on the front door and stood for some minutes. There was no answer. I walked round the building calling out. I peered through the glass of the back door. I couldn't see a soul and I noticed that there was hardly any furniture and the net curtains looked as though they'd been hanging there for years. I didn't know what to do. I'd come all this way, found out about the man in the blue van, driven to a place where he might have been and now I was stuck. I pulled the mobile out of my bag and was about to ring Rosa again when I noticed, with annoyance, that my battery was running down. I'd have to charge it up in the car. I took a last look round. There was no point in staying if there was no one to talk to. I turned and started to walk away.

I stopped when I heard the cry.

It was faint and over to my right near the building. I looked round. It was suddenly dead quiet; there wasn't a sound. A loud squawk pierced the air and I looked up to see a pair of seagulls lumbering across the sky. For a moment I thought that was what it had been; the cry of some bird in the distance. I scanned the sky and the horizon. It could also have been some child in the fields calling out.

There was nothing. The house stood mute. I turned back to my car and continued to walk away when I heard it again.

It was a female voice; calling from a distance.

I walked briskly back to the house. I was shouting, "Hello? Hello?" all the time. I put my ear to the back door. There, from somewhere in the house, was a voice shouting. I couldn't make out the words. It didn't seem to be coming from any of the rooms, it was too far away. I stood very still, hardly breathing, and willed myself to listen, to concentrate on where the noise was coming from.

When I heard it again I knew it was coming from beneath me. I looked down at my feet. There was a cellar there somewhere. That was where the voice came from.

I felt this sense of dread between my shoulderblades. I knew in that moment that Alice Tully had been abducted. I shook the back door, shouting out,

"Alice! Alice Tully!" The door was firmly locked. I heard the cries again, louder now, as though she had heard me and was trying to make contact. Possibly she was in a state of shock; maybe she had been shut up there for almost two days. I looked round the small yard and saw a pile of bricks and stones. Picking one up I stood and aimed it at the back door. I didn't have time to think about whether it was the right thing to do or not. I threw the stone with all my strength, smashing through the glass. Then I pulled my shirt sleeve over the back of my hand and carefully knocked away the remaining shards. I put my hand in and felt for the key and turned it. The door opened.

I walked straight through the kitchen into the hallway. Under the stairs was a door. There were two heavy bolts on it, one at the top and one at the bottom. All the while I could hear the girl's shouts. I undid the bolts and was faced with darkness. I felt around for a light switch and found one. A single yellow bulb hung halfway down a flight of stairs. At the bottom was another door, heavily bolted. From somewhere behind that door I could hear the voice.

For a moment I couldn't move. I was afraid to go on. Every bit of me wanted to turn round and run out of the house, back to the car and drive straight to the local police. Instead I gripped my bag tightly and walked down the stairs calling, "Alice? Alice?"

She was making a crying noise. Each step was taking me closer to her; in moments I would have the door open and she would be freed. I got to the steps near the bottom and reached out to the heavy door. I was only centimetres away from opening it when I stopped. A tiny creak from above made me look up and I froze. Someone else was there, in the house.

And then the light went out.

It was pitch black, like being at the bottom of a well. I turned to look back up the stairs but I couldn't see a thing. There was just the thunderous pounding of someone's footsteps as they came down towards me. I wanted to speak, to shout out but my words were jammed sideways in my throat and I turned and tried to open the cellar door.

A hand grabbed my hair. It pulled me roughly back out of the way and I heard a man's voice. "Bitch," he said. The bolts of the door slid back and it opened. Then with a vicious shove I was propelled into the cellar. I landed on my knees, my bag tangled up underneath me, the side of my face scraping against the ground, causing my glasses to spin off.

The cellar door slammed shut behind me.

In the corner, across the dreary room, was a faint wall light. Sitting underneath it, her hands tied up, was Alice Tully.

"Help me," the girl said.

I didn't say a word. I couldn't speak. My knees and face were grazed and there were tears in my eyes. I wasn't in any fit state to help anyone.

13

Found

I untied Alice. All the while she was crying and mumbling incoherently. When her hands were freed she brought them round in front of her and rubbed hard at the skin on her wrists. It was red and raw.

I put my arm round the teenager, and tried to comfort her. My words were guarded and half-hearted though. All the while I looked round the gloomy cellar trying to take in what had happened. A couple of minutes before I had been out in the open air, full of hope, close to finding and freeing Alice Tully. Now I was a prisoner as well. I was so sure there hadn't been anyone in the house. There had been no vehicle, no sounds, no sign of life whatsoever.

With a sick feeling I remembered the light snapping off in the cellar stairwell, the sound of heavy footsteps charging down towards me, my hair pulled viciously back until my neck was strained and sore. The man had been taller than me, a strong smell of something coming from him.

"There, there, keep calm," I said in a low voice as if I was talking to a baby.

I tried to ignore the ache on my cheek where my face had hit the floor and rubbed my free hand over my skinned knees. I'd shoved my broken glasses into my bag and screwed my eyes up to take in the surroundings. The cellar was long and narrow and had pillars in the middle. The floor looked like concrete but the walls were brick. The only light was the one behind Alice and myself, the rest of the cellar graduated into darkness. There was shelving, with old cardboard and wooden boxes stacked up. A lot of it was covered in cobwebs as if no one had touched it for years.

The air was musty and there was a faint smell of urine. If Alice had been there for two nights she must have needed a toilet. I didn't try to imagine how she had coped with her hands tied behind her back.

"Can't we go?" Alice's words emerged from her hot tearful face.

"No, not yet. Ssh…" I said calmly, stroking her hair and holding her tightly.

I wasn't feeling calm. Inside me there were the beginnings of hysteria, but I was holding it down, focusing on the girl, trying to stop myself facing up to the fact that we were both locked in the cellar of a house that was miles from anywhere.

"When will we get out?"

Alice's voice was thin and stretched. Her words crackled as though her throat was dried up. I wondered how long it had been since she had eaten or had anything to drink. Then I remembered the sandwich and water that I'd bought in the supermarket. How long ago it seemed; me walking up and down the aisles with no more to worry about than whether or not I was going to stay over at my boyfriend's house. I looked at my watch. It was almost two o'clock. How long would it be before Rosa picked up my message?

"I've got something to eat and drink in my bag," I said, lightly, forcing myself to look away from the miserable situation we were in. "Why don't we eat and then we can work out how to get out of here?"

Alice looked at me with a kind of hope in her eyes. She stopped crying all of a sudden, like babies do when they get what they want. She sat up and rubbed her eyes with her fists, smoothing her skirt down. I noticed the angry purple lines on her skin from where the ropes had been. I gave her a reassuring smile as I rummaged about in my bag. I pulled out a plastic triangle that had a chicken salad sandwich and a small bottle of water.

"Now," I said, in a businesslike way, "we'll have this and then make a plan."

Alice nodded her head and held out her hand for the water.

A little later I left her sitting up against the wall while I had a look around the cellar. It did stretch the length of the house. I walked gingerly across the floor into the shadowy area of the long room. Clouds of dust rose up from my footsteps. At the far end was a door that was locked.

"I wonder where this leads to?" I said, more to myself than for Alice.

I pulled hard at it and the door rattled loosely at the top and bottom. It was held firmly in the centre though. An old fashioned lock but no key. I continued walking around. There were shelves along one wall. On them were the kinds of things most families store away somewhere before getting rid of completely; piles of old dog magazines and newspapers, boxes of old toys and shoes, an old food mixer. All of it was covered in dust and cobwebs.

There was a workbench along the other wall and an old table and chairs that had probably been relegated to the cellar when some new furniture had been bought. Up against the wall nearest the door to the stairway were the meters that measured the gas and electricity. The gas meter was hanging off and had obviously been disconnected but the electricity meter was still going, hence the light that Alice was able to keep on.

Why would an uninhabited house have electricity, I wondered.

I was back where I'd started. Alice was sitting on the floor with her knees up to her chin. She hadn't said anything. Did she think I was measuring up the cellar with an escape plan in mind? If only it had been possible. We were below ground though, in a room with no windows and two locked doors. There was no getting out. I squatted down on the floor and took out my mobile. Even if there had been enough battery on it I wouldn't have got a signal underground.

"You remember Rosa? My boss? She knows we're here. It'll only be a matter of hours before she comes and gets us," I said with a confidence I didn't feel. If only I had actually *spoken* to her.

Alice nodded, looking in awe at me. I was her saviour, she thought. I sat down closely beside her and put my arm around her shoulder.

"While we're waiting why don't you tell me what happened?"

She looked at me, her eyes glassing over, her forehead crumbling into lines.

"In your own time." I lowered my voice. "Just what you can remember."

"It was late. Almost midnight I think. I was just gazing out of my bedroom window. I saw this van pull up in the street. I thought it might have been someone that I knew."

"Harry Smith," I said.

She carried on without commenting.

"I went downstairs and out into the street but when I got to the van it was empty. The engine was running but there was no one in the driver's seat. Then I saw the back doors were open. I went round and looked in and then…"

She stopped speaking and I imagined the scene. Alice leaning into the van and behind her a dark figure.

"I felt something go over my face. It had this awful strong smell. I must have passed out. I don't even remember being in the van. The next thing I knew I woke up here."

Her voice broke and I thought she was going to start crying again. A loud noise from above stopped her and she grabbed my arm. I tensed and held my breath. It was the sound of heavy footsteps above us. I listened hard. Then I heard the sound of the door at the top of the cellar stairs rattling.

"He's unlocking it!" Alice whispered, "He's going to let us go."

But I didn't think he was. He was checking to see that it was locked. After a couple of banging noises it went quiet again. A few moments later I heard a door slam and then it went completely silent. We both sat huddled together like that for what seemed like a long time. Alice spoke in a trembling voice.

"He'll come back soon to let us out."

I didn't say a word. I had this awful feeling. Maybe he wasn't going to come back at all.

14
Imprisoned

A few minutes later I got up and walked around again. I couldn't simply sit down and wait it out. I had to keep busy. I walked down to the far door again and gave it a pull. It rattled but stayed firmly shut. I noticed an odd smell then that I couldn't put a name to. Then I turned back and walked along the shelves looking among the items for anything that might help us. It was just junk, old stuff that nobody wanted, a child's car seat, a coolbox, an old fashioned wicker picnic-basket, boxes of nails and hinges.

I sat down and tipped out my rucksack on to the ground. I had some vague hope that there might be something in it which would prove useful; a hammer, a screwdriver even, a Swiss army knife or a set of skeleton keys.

There was nothing.

It was just past four o'clock and I'd been in the cellar for over two hours. I'd never been claustrophobic, but I was beginning to feel very uncomfortable stuck underground. Alice had been in the cellar for almost two days, yet there was no sign that any food or water had been left for her. I'd had it in mind that she'd been abducted; along with that thought was the notion that she'd been kept somewhere with the eventual idea that she would be freed. Someone wanted to keep her out of the way for a while; perhaps someone wanted to frighten her or teach her a lesson. But no food had been left for her. This began to worry me. Maybe it wasn't an abduction. Maybe it was meant to be a slow death, left without food or water in a place where she couldn't be found. The idea made my head swim and I had to push it away to keep myself from panicking.

Rosa would pick up my messages. She would be able to tell the police the name of the farm. At some point we would hear them drive up and we could call out. This would happen, I was sure. It could only be a couple of hours.

"I know who's done this," Alice said, out of the blue, her voice seeming unbearably loud in the quiet of the cellar.

"I thought you said you didn't see him?"

"I didn't, but I know who it is all the same."

I sat down beside her and took her hand. She was

only a few years younger than me and yet I felt this need to comfort her, to look after her. Her skin was warm and gritty and she moved closer and seemed to take strength from me.

"It's all a big secret, you see. If you get involved you mustn't tell anyone. No one at all. Ever. It's like you take an oath."

"What is?"

"The organization. They call themselves FAST."

"Free Animals from Slavery Today," I said.

"How do you know about them?" her voice went down to a whisper.

"I saw their leaflet in Harry Smith's office."

"Oh," Alice said.

"Are you involved with Harry?"

"No," she shook her head, "No, I'm not. He's married."

"Was Melanie?"

"Don't make me laugh. She wished she was."

"If you're not involved with him how come you've been seen with him, in his van?"

"You've been talking to Sue, haven't you? She's been spying on me."

I didn't answer.

"She thinks I killed Mel because I wanted Harry all to myself. Nothing could be further from the truth."

"Tell me the truth then," I said.

"It's a long story."

"We've got the time," I said, looking at my watch.

"I first met Harry when he was giving out leaflets at the school gates. Melanie had told me to look out for him. She liked him a lot. She was always talking about him as though she had a sort of claim on him. *Harry said this* and *Harry did that* and *Harry thinks…*"

"And you got involved in FAST? I didn't think you were into that sort of thing. I thought it was Melanie who was the animal lover."

"I'm not, not really. It's just that I was doing some work in sociology on Direct Action Groups and I just wanted to find out more about it. It sounds awful, doesn't it? I wasn't even bothered what it was for, I just wanted to write a good assignment, get a good mark."

I thought of Rosa Perks and her determination to make a good programme.

"What did you find out?"

"I saw Harry Smith a couple of times, helped him give out leaflets. Then he said he'd take me to a meeting. He told me not to tell anyone, not even Melanie. It was all so secret. I had to meet him on a corner and then, you won't believe this, but I had to be *blindfolded* until we got to the house. There were about ten people sitting round. Most of them were young people like me. No one I recognized or I've ever seen since. They were all talking about this event called Liberation Day. It was to do with this mink farm they'd discovered. You know, where they breed minks so that they can use their skins to make fur coats? Well someone had found one and they were planning to break into it and free the two thousand minks."

It was the sort of thing I'd read about on the internet.

"Anyway, later, after the meeting was over, one of the young guys pulled me and Harry over to the side and asked if we wanted to help break up this dog-fighting ring they'd found out about. There was a fight that night, he said. Harry was dead keen and just assumed that I would want to go. The others wanted to go in his van so I had no choice. I had to pretend to be really enthusiastic otherwise they might have been suspicious."

"A dogfight?" I said, thinking that that kind of stuff was all history.

"They go on all over the place. They breed the dogs for them and then they fight until the death. I know. I saw it that night."

I didn't speak. Something moved in the corner of my eye and I looked over. It could have been a mouse. I pulled up my knees and hugged my legs.

"We drove a long way. We had these balaclava things; huge woollen hats with only holes for our eyes. They kept saying to me, *Whatever you do, don't take off the hat. Keep your face covered.* It was potentially quite dangerous, they said. We had to infiltrate quickly and quietly, take notes of all the car registration numbers and then drop this smoke bomb into the middle of it."

"Smoke bomb?" I said.

"It's a chemical mix. Like a giant stink bomb really. When the container breaks smoke billows out. It stings the eyes and makes people feel nauseous."

That was what they meant by direct action. I wondered if they ever resorted to violence.

"It was out in the country. We got there about eleven. We parked on this lane and then went across a field until we got to some buildings. The fight was in the barn. It was already going on when we got there. You could hear these appalling sounds; these terrible yelps and screams and at the same time these cheers and clapping and whistling. One of the young lads went off to do the car registration plates and we skirted the place looking for somewhere to heave in the smoke bomb. Harry and me, we climbed on top of this farm machinery and looked through this gap in the wall. I could see right down into the barn where the dogfight was. There were about twenty or so blokes. They were all watching these two dogs tearing each other apart. I've never seen anything so horrible. One of them was flat on the ground but the other one was still…"

She stopped, put her hand over her mouth.

"I knew I was going to be sick. I got down and pulled my hat off. I thought I was never going to stop throwing up. Just as I looked up a group of men came round the corner. There were about six of them and they saw me doubled up on the ground. Then they saw Harry behind me on the tractor.

Harry threw the smoke bomb at them and grabbed me by the hand. We ran across the field with the others. There was a lot of commotion from behind us but they were so busy dealing with the smoke that we got a head start. We were in the van before they were anywhere near us."

"You got away."

"Yes, but I was in trouble with them for taking my balaclava off. Harry called me and told me to forget about FAST. I wasn't a member any more."

"They were afraid that someone might find you?"

"I don't think so. They were just peeved that I'd disobeyed their instructions. It's a secret and highly disciplined organization. At least that's what I put in my assignment."

"And you think they've abducted you as a kind of punishment?"

"No. It's Liberation Day today. The day they wanted to free the minks. They knew the kind of trouble I'd been in with the police, about Mel. They thought that I was going to say something about them letting the minks go."

"Was that why you were with Harry the day before yesterday?"

"Yes. He was warning me. I told him to tell FAST to get lost."

"But it wasn't Harry's van that brought you here."

"They use a lot of vans. They're keeping me here

until all the minks are released. Then they'll come and let us go. You watch."

Alice sounded calm, as though she'd convinced herself. I wasn't sure. I sat back and let the stuff she'd told me sink in. Could it be a group of animal lovers that had drugged and abducted a teenage girl? I thought of the man who had thrown me into the cellar. A big man, who'd viciously grabbed a lump of my hair and held on to it. My scalp was still aching, my face grazed and my hip-bone sore from the impact of the floor. This didn't sound like the kind of thing an animal lover would do.

"There's something else I should tell you," Alice said, quietly.

I turned to her.

"That day, when Mel was poisoned, I told you I was upstairs doing my essay?"

I nodded. All my energy seemed to have seeped away and I was feeling tired.

"I was, most of the time. But I did have a visitor."

It wasn't a surprise. I'd always felt she was keeping something back.

"Harry Smith came round. He was telling me about Liberation Day. Just keeping me in touch with things. He wasn't in the house more than ten minutes."

"Why didn't you tell the police?" I said wearily.

"I don't know. I was afraid of giving away information about FAST. I knew he didn't have anything to do with Mel's death. I was with him the whole time he was in the house. Then, when the police charged me, I was too scared to say that I'd lied. In case they thought I was lying about other things as well."

"Why are you telling me?"

"Because I trust you. Because I think you believe me when I say I didn't kill Mel."

We both lapsed into silence and sat for what seemed like a long time. I thought over the things she had told me. In some ways the whole story about FAST seemed too far-fetched to be a lie. She'd been dragged off the street and imprisoned for almost two days and two nights. Somebody was out to hurt her. It threw all the facts about Melanie's death into confusion.

At that moment, in that gloomy cellar, I was convinced that Alice hadn't killed her sister. I was too exhausted for reassurance so I squeezed her hand and told her I thought everything would be all right. The dim lighting from the bulb behind us gave the room a twilight feel and I think, after a while, I must have fallen asleep.

When I opened my eyes my head felt heavy and my mouth was dry. Alice was at the far end of the cellar looking at the door. I sat up and licked my lips. My throat felt parched. The bottle of water I had bought was empty.

"I know what the smell is," Alice said, walking unsteadily back to me. "It's coal dust."

I waited for her to reach me then I looked at my

watch. It was almost six o'clock. I'd been in the cellar for nearly four hours. I was beginning to wonder if Rosa would ever pick up my message. I had this moment of black despair where I imagined no one coming to get us. I pictured us both, a couple of days in the future, no food, no drink, no hope of being rescued.

Then I pulled myself together. Alice had been down there for two days and I had only been there a few hours. Of course Rosa would pick up my message. It was stupid to give up. Apart from anything else I had to keep strong so that Alice didn't feel afraid. I got up, dusted myself off and walked up to the far door. The smell I had noticed before was coal. That meant there was a coal cellar. It made sense. Somewhere, round the back of the house, were wooden trap doors in the ground that opened whenever the coal man delivered. Although the house hadn't been used for a long time there was probably some residue of coal there. If only we could get through the door.

"OK," I said, in a businesslike way, "we need to look along these shelves and find anything that will get us through this door. Anything heavy or sharp or even something we could wedge in and use to wrench the lock open."

I started looking back along the shelves. Alice was at the opposite end. I pulled open the wicker picnic hamper and saw knives and forks. I pulled out one of the knives and wondered if it was possible to saw my way round the lock. The knife could be sharpened on the concrete floor, perhaps, and Alice and I could take turns to saw gently through the wood. I walked back to the door, held the knife against the wood and my heart sank. It was a solid door. It would be like trying to cut through steel with a pair of scissors.

"Here!" I could hear Alice behind me.

I remembered the food mixer. Perhaps it still had a chopping blade and I could use that to get some leverage. I turned away from the door, my chest muscles tightening up with frustration. Something in my head was telling me that none of this was going to do any good.

"Look!" Alice was smiling.

"What have you found?" I said, trying to keep my voice light.

"A key," she said. "I've found a key."

15
Escape

Alice hadn't just found one key. She'd found an old plastic box that was full of them. It had once been a margarine tub, the words *Low Fat Spread* still legible on the outside. Inside there were about thirty keys, most of them rusted and old, all different types: Yales, Chubbs, padlock keys and even tiny ornate ones that might open a diary or a jewellery box.

"The key to this door might not be here," I said, dismayed.

"It's worth a try though," Alice said, frowning. "It's not like we've got much else to do, after all."

"You're right," I said, giving a big confident smile that hid a growing feeling of fear. What would happen when we'd tried all the keys and none of them fitted? What would we do then?

Alice took the box over to the light and tipped it

out on to the floor. There were eleven Chubb-type keys, at least half of which were covered in rust.

"Got any Vaseline?" she said.

"What for?" I said, puzzled.

"We can grease them. Maybe they'll go into the lock more easily."

For some reason I couldn't speak. There was a lump forming in my throat and I felt near to tears. Alice, who only a few hours before had been a gibbering wreck, had become purposeful and determined; I, who had been positive, was slowly crumbling and losing heart. I tried to pull myself together. Whether the keys worked or not, it was a plan and it would keep us going.

I knew I didn't have any Vaseline but I had something else. I rummaged about in my bag and pulled out a stick of lip salve.

"That'll do," she said and started to grease each of the keys that lay before her. As she did it I noticed the light above her flickering slightly. The dismal yellow glow of the dusty bulb was all we had. If that went out we would be in total darkness. It was not something that I wanted to think about.

The first four keys didn't fit at all. The next three did seem to fit but wouldn't turn. The eighth key was brown and flaky with rust. I held it in my fingers for a moment feeling the slipperiness of the lip salve. There were only three left to try after it. I felt myself slowing down, putting the key carefully in the lock as though I didn't want to touch the sides.

The silence in the cellar was deafening. I couldn't even hear myself breathing. When I turned the key and the lock gave a dull click I sat there in total disbelief.

The door swung towards us and the powerful, earthy smell of coal billowed out.

"It's open," Alice said, her fingers gripping on to my arm, "it's open. We can get out!"

I pulled the door so that it was open wide and put my hand over my nose to stop myself from inhaling a fog of coal dust. Alice started to cough but she walked forward anyway. I followed her up four uneven steps into the inky blackness. The faint light from the cellar spilled into the tiny stairwell but disappeared when we got up to the coal cellar itself. It was a small cavity, about the size of a child's bedroom. Once I'd adjusted to the darkness I could see that there wasn't much coal left, just scrapings that had gathered in a corner. The floor was coated with grime though, and the air seemed full of it. Alice walked to the middle and looked up. There, about three metres above, was what looked like a trap door. There was even some light that was coming through the joins in the wood and the corner which had been worn away over the years.

"It's a long way up," Alice said.

It was. Only a matter of a few metres but we still had to get up to it and open the doors to get out.

"I know," I said. "Quick, come with me."

We went down to the main cellar and between us

pulled and carried the old table over to the coal cellar. Somehow, by turning it on its side, we managed to edge it through the door and push and pull it up the stairs. Finally we got it into the space underneath the trap door. Alice climbed on top. Even by stretching her arm she still couldn't reach.

"I'll get a chair," I said.

I turned round and went back down into the main cellar. As I reached the chairs I noticed that the yellow light seemed dimmer, as though it was gradually fading back against advancing darkness in the room. I knew it could die at any minute. The bulb had probably been there for years. I moved quickly and dragged a chair across the room and up the stairs into the coal cellar. With Alice's help I got it on to the table. Holding its legs I watched as she climbed up.

"I can reach it easily," she said, pushing hard against the wood, "If I just had a bit more leverage I could push open the doors."

At that moment it went completely dark.

"What's happened?" Alice said.

The bulb had burned out.

"You stay there. I'll get something that'll give you a few more centimetres."

I walked back down into the pitch-black cellar. I put one foot carefully in front of the other, afraid of what I might fall over. I tried to remember where everything was. I got to the far wall and scrabbled around on the floor until I felt my bag. Then I stood up and made my way across to the shelves feeling around me all the time. The darkness was thick, like velvet hanging in front of me. I took each step as though I was on the edge of a cliff. Finally I touched the shelving and found what I was seeking. I carried the cool box with me to the far door and went up the steps, thankful for the few ribbons of light that came down from the trap door.

"I don't know if this will hold your weight. It might just for a few seconds…"

I put the cool box on top of the chair. Then I knelt on the wooden surface of the table and held the chair legs as firmly as I could. Alice stepped gingerly on to the top of the coolbox. She didn't speak. I could feel the tremble of the plastic as her weight settled. I was holding it all as firmly as I could but my heart was in my mouth and I was waiting for her to lose her footing and fall down.

All I heard was her puffing with exertion.

Then there was a creak and blast of grey light and a rush of air that came from outside. I looked up, squinting my eyes and there she was, sitting on the edge of the coal bunker, her legs swinging down.

"Now you," she said.

The chair wobbled more and the cool box was on the point of cracking but I stood on it anyway. I pushed myself up and she pulled me hard. In seconds the top half of my body was hanging over the rim of the trap door, my legs dangling down. With a mighty grunt Alice grabbed hold of the waistband of my jeans and dragged me over the top. In moments we were lying back on the grass in the open air, looking up at the sky.

It was nearly eight o'clock and the sun was going down. The house, the yard, the buildings, all of them were peaceful. There wasn't a soul around, not even the cry of a bird. I looked sideways at Alice and saw that she was caked with dirt. My own hands and arms were smeared with black and probably my face was too.

"Thank you," I said, feeling like a little girl.

"No, thank *you*," Alice said. "If you hadn't come I might have been down there another night."

I didn't answer. Alice still thought she was being kept out of the way while the minks were set free. In my mind it was something different altogether.

I thought we were both lucky to be alive.

16
Getting Organized

After what seemed like a very long drive I dropped
Alice off at her parents' and drove straight
round to Billy's house. It was dark, but I knew I
looked a sight and I didn't want to go home and
frighten my mum. I thought I could have a shower
at Billy's and that there was probably an old pair of
jogging trousers and a sweatshirt of mine there.

Alice didn't speak much on the way back to
London and neither did I. At first I wanted to take
her to a hospital or to the police but she wouldn't
have it. She wanted to see her dad, she said. I
decided not to argue with her. After what she had
been through she was probably better off at home. I
didn't want her to get into any further bother with
the police, and I wanted to talk to Rosa about what
had happened.

There was something else I wanted to talk to Rosa about. I had left her a number of messages and I'd been stuck in that cellar for almost six hours. She had either ignored my calls or simply not picked them up. She'd left me in real danger, not to mention Alice. I called her and yet again reached her voice mail. I gave her Billy's address and told her that if I didn't see her within an hour I was going to the police and I was going to tell them that she had withheld information.

My dad opened the front door. He was dressed immaculately in a cream linen suit as if he was about to go out. A look of shock passed over his face when he saw the state I was in.

"What's happened?" he said, looking me up and down.

"It's nothing…"

I was about to make light of it, to play it down, to shrug it off as though someone had just knocked into me and not said sorry. My bravado crumbled though and I started to cry.

"Oh Dad!"

I said it like a little girl who had just fallen over. He put his arms out to me and drew me into the hallway and sat me down on the stairs. When I looked through my tears I could see my grubby finger-marks over his pristine suit jacket. If he noticed he didn't say.

"Tell me what's happened," he said.

My dad ran a bath for me and made me stay in it for a long time. He found some TCP to clean up the graze on my face and gave me his dressing gown to wear while he toasted some bread and brewed some tea. I ate and drank ravenously. I noticed, as I was eating, that he'd changed his clothes and was wearing jeans and a T-shirt. His suit, no doubt, was ready to be taken to the dry cleaners.

"This journalist, this Perks woman, it sounds to me like someone should report her to her superior," he said, looking as though he was about to ring the radio station up himself.

"No, no. I'll deal with it."

"It was extremely dangerous; sending a teenager off to investigate an abduction without notifying the police."

"I'm not a teenager, Dad. I've been in these sort of situations before."

"It's not as if you have the resources…"

"Dad, please…"

"I just think—"

"DAD, PLEASE! LET ME HANDLE IT!"

My dad looked as though I'd just struck him.

"I'm sorry, but Mum's the one who usually gives me the third degree and I came round here to avoid it."

"It's only that I was worried about you."

The doorbell rang and he stood up stiffly. He was upset, I could tell. I shouldn't have shouted at him. I heard the front door open and the sound of rushing feet on the hallway floor. Rosa Perks burst into the room.

"Patsy, I've been worried about you."

She came across and sat down beside me, her face a picture of concern. Her cheeks were rosy and I could smell alcohol. I'd obviously caught her in the pub. From the hallway I could hear my dad rattling about. A moment later he came into the living room. He stood and looked hard at Rosa. For a horrible moment I thought he was going to say something. Then he gave me a weak smile.

"I'm just off out," he said.

I let the front door bang before I turned to Rosa.

"What happened?" she said, before I could speak. "I did try to ring you but your mobile was off."

"My battery had run down. That's what I said in the message. I told you where I was. I told you to get the police."

"I was really tied up, Patsy. Most of the day I spent working on the case!"

"I needed help, Rosa and you didn't take any notice!"

"I did hear the message. I didn't know how serious you were. When I couldn't get in touch again I thought you'd sorted it out. I'm sorry, I didn't want to call the police out in case it turned out to be nothing. Plus I was in the middle of finding all this stuff out about Frank Tully." She patted her notebook. "But you're right, I should have followed it up. I was in the wrong. I'm sorry. What more can I say?"

I didn't believe her apology. I knew she was just

trying to wriggle out of a hole. My instinct was to tell her to get lost and continue with the case myself. I owed that much to Alice Tully. But Rosa was useful. She had contacts in the police and the media that I didn't have. I had no choice but to work with her. I was also interested in what it was that she had found out about Frank Tully. I decided to get my own story out first.

In a snappy voice I told her about my day and watched as she jotted down copious notes. I went through it all: the visit to the van hire company, the false name and address, the parking ticket, the farm and finally my incarceration. I also relayed all the information that Alice had given me. When I finally explained how Alice and I had escaped she made a face of amazement.

"This is scary stuff," she said, excitedly.

"Rosa, I want to get some things clear…"

She was flicking through her reporter's notepad. It was a small fat book with rings at the top. The pages could be flipped over quickly for further notes. All I could see on the sheets that were visible were squiggles of shorthand, meaningless to me. I noticed then that she was in her regulation white T-shirt and black trousers. On her feet were some white trainers, giving her a fake casual air.

"Let me tell you my news," she said.

"Wait." I really felt that I hadn't told her off enough.

"I was meeting a contact for lunch in a pub down

by the river. You'll never guess who I saw there!"

I didn't speak. I wasn't in the mood for games.

"Frank Tully, the dead girl's *stepfather*, and Robert Dixon. Together."

"I don't get it," I said.

"Frank Tully works for the local council in the Environmental Planning Office. Robert Dixon, the man who's bought the houses that include the Pet Sanctuary? He's a builder."

I must have looked puzzled because Rosa proceeded to explain.

"The council planning office gives permission for all new building projects in the borough. A new hospital, housing estate, factory, whatever. That committee decides whether something should go ahead or not. This Robert Dixon – his company's based in Essex and it's called *Dixon Enterprises* – he bought the four Victorian houses down at Forest Walk. The council sold them at a knockdown price so that Dixon would renovate them. It's a conservation area, you see. Council policy is to restore the character of the area, thus keeping the houses in Forest Walk the way they are."

I nodded.

"But Dixon thinks of a way he can make more money. Perhaps he already knows Frank Tully or he contacts him and offers him a deal. If Frank Tully's department suspend the conservation order for Forest Walk, give Dixon Enterprises permission to tear down the houses and build luxury apartments in their place, then the value of the properties goes sky high."

It was beginning to make some sense.

"You think about it. Four houses divided into eight flats, say a million quid. But, if you knock them down and build a block of twenty luxury apartments, you're talking, three, maybe four million quid. That's a hell of a difference."

Four million pounds.

"But have you any proof?"

"No. All I know is that as soon as I saw Frank Dixon he turned pink with embarrassment. I didn't even know who Dixon was until my contact told me. Within minutes of me arriving Tully and Dixon got up to leave, their meals half eaten."

"But that doesn't prove—"

"So I went to look at the minutes of the Environmental Planning Committee and guess what? Frank Tully, who is usually known for preserving old buildings and fending off new developments, began to argue in favour of the luxury apartments. The vote was close but they won. Work starts in a couple of months."

"It's illegal though?" I said, remembering Robert Dixon harassing Wendy Smith to close the Pet Sanctuary and move out. I also remembered his flashy Rolls Royce and the nasty dog in the back.

"Only if money changes hands. If Frank Tully argued in favour of the apartments because he thought they'd be good for the area then it's legal. If however, he was paid by Dixon, now or in the future, then it's corruption and both of them could go to prison."

I sat back, finally impressed with Rosa's information. I could see its relevance to the murder.

"So, if Melanie found out about this…"

"Exactly. She could have overheard something or come across an e-mail or some papers. She may have even found some money. Don't forget, she'd have known about Dixon because of the sanctuary."

"But you're not suggesting that Frank Tully murdered his own daughter?"

"Stepdaughter. There's a world of difference. Why not? Who knows how much Dixon may have paid him. Anyway it's all speculation. What we need to do is find some more concrete evidence. It means digging through council paperwork but that's what I'm good at," she said, with typical modesty.

The speech that I was going to make about her giving me more space with the investigation didn't seem appropriate any more. I could see that she was fired up about the supposed financial wrongdoings and that was the direction that she wanted to go in. Meanwhile I could go back and continue working on the stuff that Alice had told me about; her abduction and the possible involvement of Harry Smith. There was no real point in my laying down the law because she could go off on her line of enquiry and I could do the same.

"I'm going to continue looking into the abduction. Somebody must know something," I said.

"OK," she smiled, closing her pad.

"What about the police?" I said.

"We don't need to bother them at the moment."

I nodded. I was a bit uncomfortable about not informing them about Alice's abduction. A crime had been committed, although what the intentions of the abductors were I couldn't say. On the other hand if we went to the police it would put a strain on our own investigations. I was glad that the decision was hers and not mine.

She left moments later. It seemed that there was no girl-to-girl small talk that we could manage. When Billy's front door banged shut I gave a sigh of relief. Then I got my stuff together, turned all the lights off, and left.

While driving home I put the radio on. A male newscaster was reading the midnight bulletin. The NEWS TALK jingle sounded after the headlines and then he filled in the details.

"*A mink farm in Suffolk has been broken into this evening, resulting in over a thousand minks roaming the countryside. Local farmers say that it will cause an ecological disaster, upsetting the delicate balance of countryside wildlife. NIMBUS, the owners of the farm, say that at least fifteen vandals broke in at about nine o'clock, attempted to destroy CCT video cameras and proceeded to disperse the animals.*"

A new voice came on then, fighting against background noise and crackles.

"*These people call themselves animal liberationists*

when really they are just thugs. A couple of my staff were severely traumatized by what happened here tonight. And what's the result? These minks are hand-reared. They won't be able to fend for themselves in the open countryside."

The reporter's voice came back on.

"The police say that they are keeping an open mind and any information that members of the public may have will be gratefully received."

Liberation Day had happened just as Alice had claimed it would.

17

The Wife

After a late start the next morning my mum wanted an explanation about my broken glasses and the bruises on my face. She was sitting with her arms crossed at the kitchen table as I gave an excuse about tripping over. I made light of it, saying it looked worse than it was. In fact it was painful and was making the whole side of my head ache. She didn't look as though she believed me. Gerry was next to her but he was reading a newspaper and didn't look as though he was listening.

"Those came for you earlier," she said, pointing to a bouquet of flowers on the draining board.

It was a bunch of tiny yellow roses. I picked up a card that was attached to the cellophane. *Thank you so much for finding Alice. Frank Tully*. Rosa must have been in touch with him and given him my address. It was an odd thing; a nice gesture from someone who we were investigating. It felt uncomfortable.

My mum leaned across the table and brushed some crumbs from Gerry's top. I noticed that Gerry was wearing some jogging trousers and shoes and looked very pink, as though he'd just completed a run. I had to look twice at him to make sure.

"By the way, your boyfriend, Joey, rang twice yesterday. Said to ask you if you'd meet him for lunch at the supermarket. About two, he said."

"He's not my boyfriend!" I protested.

My mum didn't speak. Her top lip curled over and her eyes bore through me. *You might fool your-self but you can't fool me*, she seemed to be saying. I got up and made myself busy washing up my mug and plate. I squirted the green liquid on and let a lather of bubbles build up. Lunch at two o'clock. It wouldn't be a bad idea to go and face Joey. I could be completely honest with him. Then perhaps we could be friends again. I rinsed the plate and cup under the running water and began to feel better. I had concrete things to do on the case and I was going to make up with Joey. I found myself smiling then stopped because of the pain.

My mum watched me with deep suspicion as I walked out of the room.

The front door of the Pet Sanctuary was open when I got there. I knocked and walked in, calling, "Is anyone there?" I was hoping to talk to Harry Smith.

I wanted to find out if Alice was right about FAST abducting and imprisoning her. She wasn't going to go to the police, I knew, but I had been imprisoned as well, and I wasn't about to let the matter drop.

Wendy Smith came down the stairs carrying a plastic bag that had the words BULK ANIMAL BEDDING on it. A few steps behind her, carrying a holdall and a shoulder bag, was Bernice, Harry Smith's wife. She was wearing orange leggings and a matching top. She looked quite striking out of her overall.

Wendy gave me an absentminded smile and continued her conversation with her daughter-in-law.

"Why don't you wait until he comes back. It's only until tomorrow. Surely you'd rather speak to him before you go?"

Bernice reached the bottom and dropped both her bags dramatically on to the floor. Then she plonked herself down on a stair.

"Hi," I said. "Sorry to interrupt. I'm looking for Harry."

"So am I," Bernice said. "Join the club."

"He's gone away for a couple of days, dear. You're the reporter, aren't you?"

"Any idea when he'll be back?"

"No, of course not," said Bernice, who fiddled with her bag and then pulled out a pack of cigarettes. "Of course I don't know when Harry will be back. You don't expect him to confide in me? I'm only his wife."

"Now Bernice, you know this is a no-smoking house."

That seemed to be the last straw. Bernice stood up, took hold of her bags and walked out of the front door. Wendy Smith tutted loudly.

"She'll be back," she said, and walked off up the hall dragging the sack of feed with her. I was left standing on my own. I could either follow Wendy or go after Harry's wife. I made a quick decision.

Bernice was halfway down the road when I caught up with her.

"Let me give you a lift," I said, puffing.

"I'm getting the tube," she said grumpily.

"I'll give you a lift to the station."

She stopped, put her bags down and pulled a lighter out of her pocket.

"Is your car a smoke-free zone as well?"

"No," I lied.

She clicked the lighter and sucked on her cigarette. I picked up one of her bags and pointed to the VW twenty metres or so away.

The underground station was only a couple of minutes' drive. I rolled the window right down and tried not to inhale the smoke. I pulled up on the kerb. Bernice had been quiet all the way.

"Are you leaving Harry?" I said.

She shrugged her shoulders and exhaled a stream of cigarette smoke which meandered slowly through the air.

"Do you know where he is?"

"He's away checking out some bigger sanctuaries. So Wendy said."

She didn't believe it and neither did I. Harry had probably been part of the group that broke into the mink farm and was, at that moment, still in Suffolk. I wondered if she knew about the extent of her husband's involvement in FAST.

"Where do you think he is?"

Her profile was very still and there was only the slightest tremble in the hand that held the cigarette. I noticed that her eyes looked a little glassy.

"Who knows? Maybe he's found a new girlfriend."

I didn't say a word. I didn't know Bernice well enough to sympathize.

"That's how he met me."

She brought the cigarette up to her mouth and then moved it slowly to the window to flick the ash outside.

"He was with this other girl when I started at the sanctuary. Laura, her name was. She was one of these high-fliers, wanted to be a vet. She had this long red hair right down to her waist. You know the sort, it had never been cut, it even had those wispy baby ends."

Bernice ran her hand through her own cropped hair. I couldn't help but finger the ends of mine.

"She was away at college and Harry loved her a lot, so he told me. Trouble was she wasn't around and he got lonely. Me and him started to spend time together, too much time. It wasn't long before I got pregnant."

"You've got a child?" I said, surprised.

"He stood by me, I'll give him that. We got married within a few weeks. Poor Laura. She made quite a scene."

I thought there was a hint of a smile around Bernice's lips.

"When I was eighteen weeks pregnant I lost the baby. By that time Laura was long gone, so Harry was stuck with me. He doesn't love me, I know that."

"Why do you stay with him?"

She threw the butt of her cigarette outside and then leant over to the back seat for her bags. I kept talking.

"You're only young. You could separate. You could find someone else. You don't have to stay in an unhappy marriage." I sounded like an agony aunt.

"Trouble is, I love him," she said, shutting the car door.

I watched her walk away, her thin legs hurrying between the heavy bags. She didn't look old enough to have left school, let alone be in an unhappy marriage. I wondered if Harry would go after her; was he bothered?

I thought about Billy and me. We'd been together for a long time. Would we get married some day? The word *marriage* had never been uttered by either of us yet some people said that we acted like an old married couple. Now he was halfway across the world and Joey Hooper was in my life. How could I even contemplate the idea of marriage with my long-term boyfriend when as soon as he'd gone I'd got together with the first attractive young man that had come along.

I pulled myself out of my thoughts and forced myself back to the present. I'd have to wait and speak to Harry Smith the next day. I turned the ignition key, intending to drive back to Sherman Street and talk to the Tully's immediate neighbours. I was going to ask them about the night Alice had disappeared. I couldn't believe that someone could snatch a girl off the street without a single person noticing something.

I took a last look at the station and was about to pull out when I saw Bernice's orange leggings coming back out and walking rapidly towards me. She was smoking another cigarette and had to stop for a couple of cars to pass by. I looked at the passenger seat to see if there was something she had forgotten. Then I rolled my window down. She came up to me, put her bags on the ground, and started to speak quickly.

"I found them together in his office. Harry and Melanie. I'd been doing the feeds and he was supposed to be working on his files. I was actually looking for her because she'd said she was going to help me bath a couple of the strays. I called out for her but she wasn't around. Then I went into his office. He had her pinned up against a wall. They were kissing and they didn't hear me. I must have stood there for thirty seconds or more. I saw him with his fingers in her hair and she had her hand up his T-shirt. Then she opened her eyes and saw me."

She stood up straight, put the cigarette up to her lips and inhaled deeply. All the while she was looking around the street. Then she bent down again.

"That was weeks ago. He promised me it was nothing, just a bit of flirting. I believed him. Then, a couple of days later I found her in the upstairs bathroom doing a pregnancy test."

"A pregnancy test?" I said, shocked.

"She tried to cover it up, but I found the receipt on the side. She bought it from Boots."

"Why didn't you come forward? It could have had something to do with Melanie's death."

"He denied it. He said it had nothing to do with him, and that if I told anyone he would be in trouble for nothing. I believed him. Like I said. I still love him."

"So why tell me?" I said, perplexed by the new turn of events.

"Because the day before yesterday he disappeared, and when I went to wash his clothes they were stinking of perfume. I don't wear perfume."

"Oh."

She threw the cigarette down and trod it into the ground with brute force. Then she raked her fingers through her short hair and took a deep breath.

"I guess it's time for me to move on," she said.

And then she walked away, more slowly this time, her bags not seeming quite so heavy. I watched until she disappeared into the underground station, an uncomfortable feeling building up inside me. Melanie was only fifteen. How could Harry Smith have been so foolish as to get involved with her?

Very possibly he knew that it was against the law to sleep with an under-age girl; could that be why he went round to Melanie's house on the Saturday she died? Perhaps Harry Smith, more than anyone else, had a reason to want Melanie out of the way.

18

Jogging Memories

I went back to Sherman Street. As I knocked on the Tullys' door I could hear the yappy dogs from next door. Did they ever shut up? I wondered.

I was keen to see Alice and sound her out about Harry and Melanie. I was sure she hadn't known about the affair but I thought the new information might prompt her to remember more about Harry's visit on the day of the murder. It might throw a new focus on it altogether.

I was out of luck though. There was no one in at the Tullys'. I decided to continue with my original plan and ask the neighbours about Wednesday night and Alice's abduction. I went to the old couple first.

It was Mr White's sister who opened the door. She was wearing the same wrap-around apron that she'd been wearing on the first day we'd spoken.

Her dogs were scurrying around her feet and she was trying to soothe them with little shushing sounds.

"I'm sorry to bother you. I'm doing some work for the Tullys' next door," I said.

"I remember you. You were here before. That dreadful business," she said.

"Miss White, is it?" I said, "And you live here with your brother, Mr White?"

"Yes, dear. Mr White is my *younger* brother."

"I just wanted to ask you about—"

"I'm seventy-nine, dear."

Miss White smiled widely.

"Really?" I said.

She put her hand out and pulled at my arm.

"Come in for a cup of tea," she said.

It was a welcome invitation. The terriers ran round and round my feet as I followed her along a dark hallway into a small room at the back of the house. She used a stick to walk, but her movements were steady and quick.

The kitchen was a place where time seemed to have stood still. In the middle was a table with a shiny chequered cloth over it. On top of it was an oven tray and a mixing bowl with an old fashioned weighing machine. A bag of flour was sitting alongside other cooking ingredients. Along the window was a big square white sink with a wooden drainer. Against the side wall was a tall cupboard that had a flap for a work surface. No units, no washing machine or dishwasher. I couldn't even see a fridge.

"I'm just starting some baking," she said, picking up an old kettle that didn't have an electric flex attached to it. "Milk and sugar?" she asked, and I nodded.

While she was filling the kettle I sat down on a chair and fussed around the dogs who jumped over and over each other to get to me. Looking up I saw a wall full of dog pictures. Some were photographs and some were paintings. How many pets could one have in a lifetime? I wondered. In seventy-nine years?

Interspersed among these were framed photographs of people. I couldn't quite make out what they were so I stood up to look closer. A group of men were lined up and smiling at the camera. One of them I recognized as Miss White's brother. *PDSA Charity Fayre 1995*. Another photo had Mr White and his sister holding a giant cardboard cheque that said *Pay Friends of Essex Dog Rescue, One Thousand Pounds Only*. A third had Mr White on his own, holding a plaque which I couldn't read. Underneath it said, *Star Fund-raiser 1998*.

"My brother is a great fund-raiser," Miss White said, pouring boiling water into a teapot that was the shape of a cottage with a thatched roof.

"So I see," I said. I remembered that he'd also raised money for the Pet Sanctuary.

"He has so much more energy than me. There's a seventeen-year gap, you see. Our mother had him late. I looked after him a lot when he was a child. Now he looks after me." She placed a woolly tea cosy over the top of the teapot. "Come, while the tea's brewing I want to show you something he made for me."

I glanced at my watch, not really wanting to spend too much time with the Whites. I still had the other neighbours to talk to.

"We've had eleven dogs, over the years," Miss White continued. "They're such good company, you see. They give you this unconditional love."

I followed her out of her back door and into the garden. She was striding ahead of me, her two Yorkies running back and forth and jumping up at her knees at the same time. As I was walking I took a look back at the houses. I could see the Tullys' back door. The garden fences on both sides were low wooden ones, and there were gaps where time and the elements had worn away the wood. It wouldn't be hard, I thought, to squeeze through from garden to garden. Any reasonably fit person could do it.

Miss White had come to a sudden halt. I stopped too and was faced with a large bed of haphazard flowers, in the middle of which were several small wooden plaques. I looked at the old lady for some explanation.

"It's where our dogs rest," Miss White said, pointing at the area.

And then it dawned on me. The plaques had names on them: Lolly, Bertie, Postie, Molly and Tipper. There were others but they had faded with time. It was a pet cemetery.

"How nice," I said, not sure if I meant it or not.

"We look after them, you see. They're with us always."

I was struck then at how dramatically different people could be. Here were an old couple who had given their lives to the care of animals. Only the previous day I had heard from Alice the story of other people whose pleasure it was to see animals tearing each other to bits. How could people be so unlike each other?

I pushed these dark thoughts out of my mind as we walked back to the house. In the kitchen I got back to the subject of my visit.

"Both you and your brother were here on the day that Melanie was killed?" I said, in a chatty way.

"We were. Mr White was working on his computer and I was doing some cooking."

"A computer?" I said, surprised. It seemed incongruous to have a computer in such an old-fashioned place.

"Mr White's company gave it to him so that he could work at home. He's an insurance adviser. He's helping to set up – what do you call it? – internet insurance."

She handed me a tiny china cup and saucer. I smiled. A seventy-nine year old woman talking about the internet was downright odd.

"I really wanted to ask you about last Wednesday night…"

"My brother is very conscientious, dear. He was working all that terrible day. He might have taken the dogs out for a little walk but mostly he was in his room. We were so shocked."

"And Wednesday, just before midnight? Might either of you have seen anyone hanging round the street?"

I could hear the front door opening.

"That's Mr White, dear." The old lady smiled.

After a few moments Mr White appeared in the kitchen. I wondered if his sister called him by such a formal title all the time.

"Who's this?" he said, looking at me. "Ah, you're the young lady I was speaking to the other day."

"Yes. I've just called round to…"

"We're just talking about that sad business next door," Miss White said.

"Actually, I really wanted to ask about Wednesday night. Late, about eleven-thirty?"

Mr White took off a light zip-up jacket. Underneath he had a short-sleeved shirt with a tie and a sleeveless V-necked pullover.

"There was an incident on Wednesday night. I just wondered if either of you saw anything."

"I was out until quite late," Mr White said.

"I was in bed by ten. I'm always in bed early," Miss White said, looking curious.

"You might have noticed a blue Ford van parked in the street?"

"I usually have the curtains drawn." Miss White said.

"I don't think I got back until after one."

Mr White turned his head away and coughed lightly into his hand.

"Forty years of smoking cigarettes. Not good at all. Here, have one of these." The old lady pulled a white paper bag out of her apron. Mr White gave a defeated look and took a sweet out of it. Then she offered one to me. It didn't seem right to refuse.

"Pear drops," Miss White said. "My brother's favourite."

I stood up. I'd been there almost an hour and neither of them had seen anything. It was time to go.

"I'll show you out, dear," Miss White said, seeming to read my mind.

Outside I found myself tense, my neck muscles tight. I moved my shoulders round and shook my arms to help myself relax. Then I went along and knocked on a couple more doors. Nobody had seen a thing. The last house I knocked on was directly across from the Tullys'.

A young blonde woman opened the door. She remembered me from the previous time I'd called. She had a toddler wedged on her hip who was eating a biscuit. He offered it to me as I explained why I was there.

"I did see a blue van," the woman said. "I thought it was the girl's boyfriend. I've seen it round here before."

"You didn't see the driver?" I said, smiling at the small child who was looking at me with saucer eyes.

"Nope, I was trying to get this one back to sleep."

I thanked the woman and walked back across the road. I stood in front of my car for a moment and looked again at the Tullys'. Through the net curtains I was sure I could see a shape at the living-room window. A woman was staring out into the street. She was facing in my direction, still as a statue. It was Sue Tully. I wondered if she had been there when I was knocking or if she had come back while I was talking to the Whites. I felt I ought to wave or make some gesture, yet it seemed a trivial thing to do. I wasn't a friend, or even an acquaintance. On top of that I was at odds with her. She thought her step-daughter was guilty and I was trying to prove her innocent. I was also about to investigate her husband. In my embarrassment I fiddled with my bag and pretended I hadn't noticed her.

When I got to my car I drove straight off without looking back. The radio came on automatically with the news. It was two o'clock. I remembered then the arrangement Joey had made for him and me to meet for lunch. *At the supermarket*, my mum had said, *about two*.

I'd completely forgotten about it. I pulled out my mobile phone to ring him and then stopped. If I saw him it would only mean rehashing the whole argument. Even though I hadn't meant to let him down, it might be better to just leave it. I put my phone away and continued driving.

19

Harry Smith

My plan was to go and see Harry Smith on Sunday morning. I got up about nine and found my mum in the kitchen, her face like thunder.

"Gerry's sleeping it off. He had too much wine last night."

Her lips were pursed together, as though she was afraid she might say something she would regret. I took a mug from the drainer to make myself a cup of tea.

"Honestly, over the last few weeks Gerry's been really odd," she said, a look of puzzlement on her face.

"Um," I said, putting a tea bag into my cup.

"What do you mean?" my mum said.

Gerry was doing DIY work around the house, he was taking more care with his clothes, he'd started jogging. At the same time he had lost some of his humour and was drinking more wine than usual. He was jealous of my dad. I knew it and he knew it. How could my mum not know?

"You do mean something. Come on, out with it. Has Gerry spoken to you?"

Don't get involved, I kept saying to myself.

"Patsy!" my mum said, threateningly.

"Well, do you think that Gerry is a little unsettled by Dad?"

"Your dad? What's he got to do with anything?" she said, angrily.

I closed my eyes with irritation. Now my mum was going to fight with me instead of Gerry. My original instincts had been right, stay out of other people's arguments.

"I don't know!" I said holding my hands up. "It's just a suggestion."

I picked up my mug of tea and walked smartly out of the kitchen. I could hear my mum's irritation in her heavy breathing. As I passed their bedroom I could hear the low growl of a snore. It would be quite a while before Gerry was able to respond to her.

Once in my room I decided to write to Billy. It wasn't actually my turn to send a letter, but I wrote one anyway. I explained to him about my dad coming back and staying at his house and the effect it was having on my mum and Gerry. I also said a few things about the case but not too much. I asked him about what he was doing and whether he might be able to come home for a short break as he had suggested in his last letter. At the end I sent my love and filled a whole line with kisses.

I hadn't mentioned Joey Hooper at all.

I heard footsteps come up the stairs and my mum's bedroom door open. I had half-thought that I might get out all the stuff about the case, lay it flat on my bed and see if I could pull it together. I was on edge, though. I could hear my mum moving about in her bedroom next door, her voice like a pair of scissors cutting through the silence of the room. I felt tension in the back of my neck.

I decided to write to Joey and explain. I got out some lined paper from my rucksack and wrote my address at the top. *Dear Joey*, I wrote, *I'm really sorry I missed lunch yesterday. I was interviewing possible witnesses and I just didn't notice the time...* I continued telling him how much I liked him but how I was committed to my relationship with Billy. I ended it weakly by saying that I hoped we could still be friends.

I addressed both letters. Billy's was a small blue air-mail envelope and my writing seemed to fill the front of it. The words kept to a straight line and there seemed more loops than usual, making the address look decorative, playful. I put Joey's into a brown envelope that I had taken from the office. The words sat in the middle of an acre of space and seemed tightly slanted to the left. It looked mean, like a bill or a reminder to visit a dentist.

I heard a loud voice from next door. It was my mum. Then I heard Gerry's low murmur in reply. There was going to be a row, I could sense it in the air. I did not want to be around. I picked up my bag and my letters and decided to go out.

Even though it was still early I decided to head up to the Pet Sanctuary. I stopped and posted my letters and then took a leisurely drive in the direction of Loughton, thinking about the case as I went.

For the past week I'd been keen as mustard to get away from my uncle's agency; to be working as a kind of journalist, to be in an office with other people, girls of my own age. To do something different. It hadn't turned out like that though. I'd ended up finding myself increasingly frustrated at the way the case was being handled. The more time I spent in Rosa Perks' company the more confused I got. Not only did I think she wasn't sincere, I also didn't like the about-turns she took. Whenever there was the slightest bit of evidence against somebody she had them hung, drawn and quartered. Instead of the case becoming clearer it was getting more complex.

Now she thought it might be part of a financial scam. I wasn't convinced. I was placing my bet on love – or the lack of it – being a strong enough motive for murder.

It took about twenty minutes to get there. The sanctuary was closed so I rang the bell. After a few moments the door opened and Harry Smith was in front of me. He scowled when he saw me.

"Can I have a word?" I said, walking briskly past him into the hallway.

"I thought we'd had our conversation."

"There's been some developments," I said, with a sickly-sweet smile.

"I haven't got time for this…"

I could hear a number of footsteps along the hallway accompanied by a hoarse wheezing sound. Wendy Smith was holding a large dog by the lead.

"Oh," she said, "I thought it was Dixon."

"It's OK. She's going now," he said.

I stood my ground.

"I thought we could use a bit of privacy to discuss your relationship with Melanie," I said, raising my eyebrows in the direction of his mother. His face took on a look of extreme annoyance.

"Is everything all right?" Wendy Smith said.

"It's OK Mum, I'm just going to clear up a few things."

He opened the door and walked out into the front garden. I followed him. He leant against the garden wall and looked moodily up and down the street, his laboured breaths suggesting annoyance. I didn't care.

"You were having an affair with Melanie Tully. Your wife caught the two of you together. Then Melanie thought she was pregnant. Do you know what the police would say if they knew about this?"

"*Please*," he said. "Melanie was a sweet girl but she had an active imagination. I was her friend."

"And the pregnancy?"

"She was not pregnant. That much you must know is true."

He was right. The pathology report on the dead girl had not said she was pregnant.

"She bought a pregnancy test. That means she *thought* she might be. People don't usually think they might be pregnant unless they're doing something to bring it about."

"I know what you're implying and I'll admit that we kissed and cuddled a few times but it was never any more than that. The rest of it, the pregnancy stuff, it was all in her imagination. We were just friends."

I was suddenly reminded of the conversations I'd had with Joey. *We're just friends*, I'd said, over and over. No wonder Joey had been so incredulous. I, for one, didn't believe Harry Smith for a minute.

He was quiet and looked smug. It was his word against the word of a dead girl. Bernice had seen them kissing but that, at least, wasn't against the law. I looked away for a moment. In the distance, coming down the road towards us, I could see the turquoise Rolls Royce. I carried on.

"On the day that Melanie was killed you went round to her house. Why?"

"Who told you that?" he said, looking at me suspiciously.

"Alice."

He looked surprised, as though he hadn't expected Alice to tell anyone.

"Why were you there?"

"I went to talk to Alice," he said, flustered.

"About FAST and the mink farm?"

"Did she tell you this?"

"She holds you responsible for her abduction."

"Her what?" he said, his eyes looking past me. I turned and saw Mr Dixon parking his Rolls Royce opposite the sanctuary. In the back was the slavering dog that I'd seen before. Its nose was poking out of a tiny slit of window. I continued talking.

"She spent over two days tied up in a cellar. She thinks your people from FAST were behind it. Unless, of course, you think it was all in her *imagination.*"

Mr Dixon was out of his car. He gave us a tight smile and walked up the path to the front door. It opened immediately, as though someone had been waiting for him to arrive. I heard Wendy Smith's voice welcome him brightly. I felt Harry Smith tense beside me as the front door closed.

"Did you know about the abduction?" I said, trying to put Dixon out of my mind for the moment.

"What am I? Public Enemy Number One? So far, you've accused me of having sex with an under-age girl and then murdering her, and now I'm supposed to have abducted her sister."

Putting it like that did make it sound far-fetched. I didn't flinch though. I've seen people convincingly deny their part in a crime and the next day calmly admit to it. I didn't answer him either. I just stood silent, giving him room to speak.

"I don't even have to talk to you," he said, wearily. "You're not the police. I had nothing to do with Melanie's murder. Why pick on me?"

"Because she threatened to go to the police about you and her?" I was guessing.

Just then the front door opened and Dixon strode out. This time his smile was wider, almost gleeful.

"Goodbye, Mrs Smith. It's been nice to do business with you at last," he shouted.

Passing us he gave a mock salute. I said nothing and Harry Smith simply stared at him. As soon as Dixon had got back into his car and moved off the young man walked abruptly away from me and back into his house. I followed.

Wendy Smith was sitting on the bottom stair holding a cheque.

"What have you done?" Harry said.

"I've accepted a donation," she said and stood up. She walked across to the pinboard, and taking a drawing pin she stuck the cheque up. "It means we have to move out in a week."

"We can't!" Harry said.

"We can. Ring up Bernice and get her to come back. She's a good worker."

Wendy Smith walked off up the hallway humming to herself.

"As I was saying," I said, trying to hold on to the threads of my interview, "some people will think that Melanie was threatening to tell about the affair."

"There was no affair!"

Harry Smith rolled his eyes as though he was at the end of his patience. There was real anger beneath the irritation. Whether it was with me or the cheque that had been carelessly pinned to the board, I didn't know.

"What about Dixon?" he said, pointing out towards the street. "Why don't you ask him? He had a good enough reason to want Mel out of the way."

"Melanie told you about Dixon?"

"And her stepfather. Thick as thieves the both of them. Not that you'll ever prove it. His sort never leave any proof."

We both looked at the cheque on the board. It was made out to Wendy Smith and signed by Robert Dixon. On top of it was a slip which said, *With Compliments, Dixon Enterprises, Millennium House, Ilford, Essex.* I stepped closer and saw the amount. *Twenty-thousand pounds only.* It was months before Wendy Smith had to move. If she went in the next week Dixon could start on his luxury apartments sooner. The payment wasn't illegal. There was no proof that it was anything other than a kind donation to a local pet charity. I stopped looking and forced myself back to the important subject; the day that Melanie died.

"You were there in Melanie's house an hour or so before she ate the poison. You've kept this fact back from everyone. You must admit that that looks suspicious."

"What about Dixon? He was in Sherman Street. Probably for just the same reason that he came round here. To deliver some dirty great cheque."

"Dixon was there?"

"Dixon probably went prepared. In one pocket he had a cheque, in the other the poison."

"No one said Dixon was there."

"I saw him as I left. I was starting the van up and he pulled into a space a couple of houses along."

"Someone would have noticed the Rolls."

"He wasn't in the Rolls. He was in a dark saloon car. A BMW."

"So after you came out he went in? How come you didn't tell the police about this?"

"They never asked me."

I was silent, letting it all sink in. That much was true. The police hadn't asked Harry Smith anything because they hadn't known he was there in the first place. Alice hadn't told them. The other person who hadn't said anything was Frank Tully. If Dixon had visited he must have known about it. It meant that the house in Sherman Street had been busy that day.

And one of those visitors had most probably killed Melanie Tully.

20

Business Matters

I waited until the next day to go and see Frank Tully. Rosa had told me to keep calm and take my time. She still had a lot of paperwork to sift through before either of us could accuse him of anything concrete. At the moment he was still a grieving parent, she said.

After a bit of small talk I asked him about his relationship with Robert Dixon. He didn't flinch. After being seen in the pub by Rosa he had probably been expecting the question.

"Robert Dixon is a builder who I've known for years."

He was sitting on the sofa. He was wearing a suit and tie and had been about to go out to work as I arrived. He seemed irked to see me and mumbled something about being late for an appointment. I'd smiled cheerfully and said I wouldn't be long.

Sue Tully was still in her dressing gown, slumped in an armchair, as far away from her husband as it was possible to be. There was a smell of cooking in the air and in the distance I could hear music from a radio. I asked her how she was and she jerked her head up and down. Alice was out and neither of them knew where.

I asked Frank Tully what his role on the Environment Committee was and how that fitted with his relationship with Dixon. He didn't seemed put out at all.

"In my job you get to know builders and architects; it's part of the territory. There's nothing untoward in that. If you're asking why I argued in favour of the apartments in Forest Walk, I'm quite happy to explain. Twenty luxury apartments will bring well-off people into the area. They'll pay their council tax and shop for their goods and services locally. The area is full of Victorian houses, most of which adhere to the conservation by-laws. A balance is what we're looking for, Miss Kelly; respect for the past and good economic sense."

Rosa had known he would respond like this. *He'll deny it and there won't be any evidence*, she'd said. *The money probably changed hands in a brown envelope. My guess is it's in a safe-deposit box somewhere and it can't be traced. That's how these local government scandals work.*

"I've done nothing illegal. Sue will back me up."

We both looked at his wife but she didn't speak.

"She's still very traumatized," Frank Tully said,

wearily. He rubbed hard at the bridge of his nose. "This has been a terrible strain on everyone."

Sue Tully gave a sudden shuddering sob. Then she pulled herself up out of the chair and walked slowly to the door. Frank Tully rose up to go after her but she held her hand out to stop him.

"I want to be on my own," she said, flatly, and left the room.

"It takes time," he mumbled and then turned back to me.

"Did Melanie find out about this?"

"About me doing my job? She was always going on about the environment. She didn't like any new building project. And she hated Dixon."

He looked at his watch and began to brush down the fabric of his trousers.

"Mr Tully, can you tell me why Robert Dixon visited this house on the day that Melanie was murdered?"

He looked surprised.

"I have a witness who says he drove into the street and parked his car round about two o'clock."

"Well, yes, he did. He was picking me up. We had some matters to discuss."

"Why didn't you tell the police that he came? Even if it was only to pick you up?"

"Strictly speaking he didn't come to the house. I was waiting for him. I saw his car so I went out to him. You can ask my neighbour. He was coming in with his dogs as I was going out. I passed the time of day with him then I walked on. Dixon never came anywhere near the house."

"But you still didn't feel it was something you could tell the police?"

He stood up.

"Miss Kelly, I appreciate that you and Rosa Perks are trying to prove my daughter didn't kill her stepsister. I'm also very grateful that you were able to find my daughter when she went missing. You seem like a very bright and brave girl."

I groaned inwardly at his use of the word *girl*.

"But I really do feel that you're barking up the wrong tree here. My stepdaughter Melanie did know about my friendship with Robert Dixon. She also knew that I was arguing in favour of the apartment block. She wasn't happy about it, I grant you. But are you seriously suggesting that Robert Dixon would come here and poison Melanie because she disagreed with him?"

"No, not because she disagreed with him, but because she was threatening to go to the police?"

I was speculating. I had no idea what Melanie had said or done.

"This is rubbish," he said, standing up.

I stood up as well. That was when I noticed a creeping redness up his neck. The rest of him in his suit, shirt and tie was calm, but from under his collar came what looked like a deep pink blush.

"I must be going. I have an appointment at nine forty-five."

"Can I give you a lift?" I said.

"No thanks."

I followed him out to the hall where he picked up his keys and mobile phone. He walked out the front door and then had to step back in to get his briefcase which was on the floor by the banisters. He tutted and picked it up. Then he waited for me to walk out ahead of him before he called up to his wife.

As I was getting into my car I watched him stride briskly up the street. I didn't have time to follow him but I was willing to place a bet on the fact that he would meet Dixon some time soon. Whether that fact was significant or not I didn't know. I started up the car and drove towards the NEWS TALK offices.

Rosa wasn't depressed by my information.

"You didn't expect him to confess, did you?" she said, brightly.

She was wearing a long black dress with short sleeves. Around her neck were some white beads that matched her earrings. I wondered why she always stuck to black and white. I was wearing some beige linen trousers and a dark blue T-shirt. When I'd put it on that morning it had looked quite smart but the trousers were already lined with creases. Up against Rosa's flowing skirt and her perfect jaw-length hair I looked positively hippyish.

On Rosa's desk I noticed two files. They were brand new with small labels on the corners. One had the letters FAST on it and the other had

DIXON ENTERPRISES. She saw me looking.

"Just organizing my papers," she said, smiling.

A knock on the door sounded. One of the girls from the office popped her head in.

"Rosa, I've got some stuff for you," she said, giving me a quick smile.

"I'll be back in a minute, Patsy. Help yourself to some coffee. Maybe you could pour me one as well."

Rosa pointed over in the corner and I looked round to see a stylish glass coffee percolator and two matching mugs. When the office door closed I went over and poured coffee into both of the mugs. I put Rosa's down, blew across the top of mine and picked up a piece of paper that was by the phone. In the top corner were the words *Birch Farm, Abbeyfield, Essex*.

It was the address of the farm where Alice had been imprisoned. Rosa must have been trying to find out where the owners were. *Birch Farm and Kennels*. It took me back for an instant; the quiet countryside, the deserted house, the broken back window, the smell of coal. I'd been underground for six hours and at the time it had seemed like six days. Looking back, though, the time seemed to have passed in a flash. Then I had been seriously afraid; now it seemed like an adventure. I put my hand on my knee where it had been bruised and felt no soreness. I'd even forgotten about my face.

Truthfully, I'd hardly thought about it much since it happened. I'd been absorbed in the case. Trying to prove Alice innocent had become a thankless job.

Her stepmother was hostile, her father was covering up his own wrongdoings and the journalist who had wanted to highlight an injustice was just about to jump ship on to an altogether more juicy case.

Rosa came back smiling from ear to ear.

"Have you seen Robert Dixon?" I said, remembering that he was the one person who we'd not actually spoken to yet.

"That's what I wanted to talk to you about. I went over there this morning."

"And?"

"It's one of those big buildings that lease office space. There must be twenty different companies there. Dixon's is on the fourth floor. The man himself was actually out on site somewhere so I chatted to the receptionist and got a general feel of the place."

"Oh," I said.

"Anyway, that's not what I wanted to tell you. After I'd finished I left the office and was standing waiting for the lift when I glanced around the corridor. Just next door to Dixon Enterprises is Crown Brokers."

She looked at me as though she'd just said something significant. I didn't speak, wondering what I was missing.

"Hello?" she said and banged her knuckles on her skull as though trying to see if anyone was in.

"Sorry?" I said, densely.

"Mr Raymond. The man who hired the van that Alice was abducted in. He said his insurance was with Crown Brokers? Remember?"

I did remember. I'd rung up and spoken to a man who denied any knowledge of Mr Raymond. He'd been unhelpful and grumpy.

"And Crown Brokers turns out to be next door to Dixon Enterprises?"

I thought about it for a minute.

"Maybe it's just a coincidence?" I said, unenthusiastically.

"*Please*. There are hundreds of insurance companies. The one that has a link to this case is next door to the builder who just happens to be connected to the dead girl!"

"What does it prove?"

"That Dixon is in some way connected with the murder and the abduction? That these events are all linked to local government corruption?"

"But what about FAST?"

"I've not ruled them out!"

Rosa picked up the file that had the letters FAST on it. She opened a drawer and pushed it in. The other file, the one with DIXON ENTERPRISES written on it, stayed on top of the desk.

"Go and see Alice Tully. See if she can remember anything new about the abduction. Ask her whether Melanie ever said anything about Dixon to her. If we could link the builder with the abduction we may have something concrete."

FAST had been quite literally filed away. Rosa had decided that it was all about Dixon. I had yet to be convinced.

21
Letters

When Sue Tully opened her front door she was fully dressed. She'd washed her hair and put some lipstick on and looked a lot better than when I'd seen her earlier. She smiled when she saw me and put her hand on my arm and pulled me into the house.

"I just wondered if Alice was back in," I said, surprised at her friendliness.

"I've got something to show you," she said, looking excited.

"Is Alice still out?" I said.

She didn't answer, she just walked up the stairs and beckoned to me to follow.

I felt uncomfortable with Sue Tully, I have to admit. Of all the people involved in the case she seemed to be the one who was hurting the most. Her daughter had been killed and she herself had found her. She strongly believed her stepdaughter had been responsible for the murder. Her husband couldn't share her grief for Melanie or her certainty about Alice's guilt. I wondered how long the marriage would last. If the charges were dropped against Alice then she would be upset; if Alice was convicted then he would be upset. It was a situation in which nobody won.

At the top of the stairs Sue Tully went into a bedroom.

"It's Alice's," she said.

I held back, not wanting to go into Alice's room when she wasn't there.

"Don't worry, Alice won't come back. She's out with her boyfriend. The one I told you about. I know, I followed her out of the street and she got into his van."

"You don't mean Harry Smith?" I said.

"I told you they were involved," she said.

I felt perplexed. What was Alice doing with Harry? After spending two days and nights in that cellar, surely Harry would be the last person she wanted to see.

"I've got something to show you," she said, pulling at me.

The room was tidy, although the bed was still unmade and there were some clothes hanging over the back of a chair. A computer sat on a desk in the corner and there were small piles of books and papers around.

"Here," Alice Tully said, pointing to a piece of paper that was lying on the unmade bed.

I went reluctantly forward and glanced in the direction of the paper. I really felt like I was trespassing and had no right to be there. Sue Tully plucked it up and waved it towards me.

"I found it wedged in her mattress. It was well hidden," she said.

It was a letter. Glancing at the bottom of the page I could see that it was from Harry Smith. At the top were the words *Dearest Alice*.

"Read it," Sue Tully said. "Go on, read it."

I started at the beginning.

Dearest Alice, it said, *Last night, after I dropped you home, I drove round and round trying to sort out the situation we are in. The one important thing in all this mess is that I love you.*

What happened between Melanie and me was a big mistake. I was in an unhappy marriage and I didn't know how to get out of it. I felt sorry for Melanie and got involved. As soon as I met you I knew I'd been stupid.

I intend to tell Bernice about us. It's not fair on her to keep her hanging on when I don't love her.

I saw Melanie this morning and she is threatening to go to the police. She says she will tell them that she might be pregnant. It's all nonsense, of course, but she could cause a lot of trouble for me and for the sanctuary. I honestly don't know what to do.

There must be a solution. All I know is that I love

you and I hope that soon we will be together. Love Harry.

"Look at the date!" Sue Tully said.

I looked. It was the day before Melanie was poisoned.

"Now do you believe me!" she said, a look of triumph in her eye.

"Can I take this letter?" I said.

"If you promise you'll take it to the police," she said.

The strangest thing happened then. She turned around and started to make the bed. She seemed to be humming to herself. After she'd straightened the duvet and puffed up the pillows she moved on to the desk and started to close opened books and put various pens and pencils into a desk tidy. She seemed to have forgotten I was there.

I backed away and went down the stairs holding the letter. I hadn't promised her I would take it to the police. I knew Rosa wouldn't want that.

I drove halfway home and pulled into a McDonald's Drive-Thru. The car park was half-empty so I sat in the driver's seat with the door open and chewed quietly on some fries and a burger. After the first couple of bites I put the burger down. My appetite had gone.

Alice Tully had lied to me about Harry Smith. She'd said she wasn't involved with him. *He's married!* she'd said, affronted, when I'd asked her. Alice had done quite a lot of lying one way and another. At first she'd said she was on her own all day in the house. Then she admitted that Harry Smith came round to talk to her about FAST. She'd told lies to the police and to her dad and stepmum. What I wasn't sure about was whether she'd told the biggest lie of all.

Had she, in fact, killed her sister?

I looked across the car park at the entrance of McDonald's. It was all dark wood with leaded windows, the yellow M looking ever so slightly out of place. A group of young boys went in, four of them, in white shirts and school ties, their bags slung over their shoulders. They were laughing and joking, pushing each other from side to side. One of them had to stand back at the door because someone was coming out. It was a young black girl in shorts and a sleeveless T-shirt. Behind her, carrying a take-away bag of food, was Joey Hooper.

I ducked down, not wanting him to see me. He'd turned and walked in the other direction anyway, the girl walking along happily beside him. I strained my eyes in the distance to see if she was holding his hand or whether he had his arm around her. There were too many people in the way though and I sat down feeling thoroughly disgruntled.

What had I hoped for? That he would pine away in his bedroom, sick at heart because we weren't a couple any more? I knew he wouldn't. Joey Hooper was a bright, attractive kid who wasn't dependent on me for company.

I stayed where I was until I was sure that he and the girl had disappeared from sight. Then I took my half-eaten burger and fries and chucked them into a nearby bin, and drove off.

At some point, during the drive home I forced myself to stop thinking about Joey and go back to Alice Tully. I pictured her as I had seen her in the cellar, dirty and dishevelled. *I think you believe me when I say I didn't kill Mel*, she had said. She had been sure that the animal activists were behind her abduction. But how could that be the truth if she was having a relationship with Harry Smith? Had the whole thing been a ruse?

I remembered the day she had disappeared. Frank Tully had not wanted to inform the police. He knew that she might have broken her bail conditions, he said. He didn't want her to get into more trouble. Was that the reaction of a normal father? Or had Frank Tully seen his daughter voluntarily get into that blue van?

I went back to the beginning and tried to work out what might have happened. I tried to imagine Alice, with Harry's help, putting the poison on top of the pasta. It was a hard picture to pull together. The only explanation I could think of was that Harry and Alice had not meant for Melanie to die; possibly it had been an attempt to distract her from her threats to go to the police. The glass container might have been put in Alice's bag for disposal. In the event, once Melanie had died, it had been forgotten about until discovered by the police the next day.

Once Alice had been charged with the murder the two of them concocted a plan for Alice to disappear. If Alice had packed her clothes or left in any planned way it would simply have added to her guilt. So they decided that she would simply vanish off the street. Harry Smith hadn't used the Pet Sanctuary van but he'd got another one that looked identical. Hence if he had been seen anywhere it wouldn't have looked out of place.

Alice could have lived in the farm for weeks or months before anyone noticed. During that time people would have drawn the conclusion that she had been killed and perhaps the murder of Melanie would have turned into a bizarre double killing of two sisters. Once the Pet Sanctuary had moved premises Harry Smith could quietly disappear and he and Alice could go off together.

Except that Sue Tully had taken part of the registration number and I had found the earring in the back of the van. Perhaps Alice and Harry had hatched a contingency plan. If they were seen or followed or discovered then Alice would pretend she had been abducted and held against her will. How perfect to say that it was FAST who had done it. With such a secret organization how could any-one find out if it were really true or not? Alice had even called out for help; it was the only thing she could have done. Once I had found the farm it would only be a matter of time before the police came.

I thought back to the hours I spent in the cellar with Alice. She had been tied up tightly, her wrists red-raw. Could Harry have done that to her? Was it Harry who had pushed me into the cellar? And yet Alice had seemed so upset, so sincere. She had confided in me about the dogfight. Was even that true?

Then I remembered. As time had gone on it had been me who had been on the brink of giving up. She had kept me going. Her spirits had been high. At the time I had put that down to the fact that she thought she was being held by FAST. But it could have been that she knew Harry was there outside somewhere, ready to open the door if we couldn't find our own way out.

It came to me then that it was she who had found the all-important box of keys. *I've found a key*, she'd said, smiling with sheer delight. Had that all been a lie?

I turned into my own street and parked my car. I'd driven all the way from McDonald's without really registering the roads, the turns, the traffic lights. I'd drifted into a kind of daze thinking about Alice and Harry. I'd even forgotten about Joey Hooper sharing a McDonald's lunch with a new girl.

I took Alice's letter indoors and found, on the table, a blue airmail envelope addressed to me. It was from Billy. It must have crossed over with the letter I had sent the previous day. I held it up to my chest. After the last few hours I needed something to cheer me up. I decided to make myself a cup of tea and take the letter up to my room to read.

While the kettle was boiling I tried to think of Billy in Africa at that very moment. He would probably be wearing old shorts and a T-shirt, with trainers or boots on. Maybe he would be with some of his co-workers or some of the local lads who he teamed up with. He could be sharing a joke with them or showing them how to put together some piece of machinery. He might even be playing football. I smiled to myself. When he lived in London he had no interest in sports whatsoever. Now his letters were full of football and table tennis and cricket.

I poured the boiling water on to my teabag and took a deep breath.

I was feeling sorry for myself. My boyfriend was having a full and meaningful life in an exotic location while I was stuck in London in the middle of a case that was becoming nastier by the day. I had just discovered that the girl who I'd risked my life to find had in all probability been lying to me and taken me for a fool. My mum and her new husband were going through a bad patch and my substitute boyfriend had given me up without a backward glance.

I needed cheering up.

I took the letter upstairs with my cup of tea and

sat down on my bed and opened it. The first words hit me like a blast of cold air.

Dear Patsy, I don't know how to tell you this but I've met somebody else. She's one of my co-workers and her name is Sandy. We were just friends at first but now things have developed…

My throat went dry as dust as I continued to read. The letter went on for pages it seemed. Words like *love* and *affection* and *compatibility* seemed to jump up at me. Phrases like *it's for the best … we've both moved on … we can still stay friends* stood out like bits of driftwood in an empty sea. My eyes swept back and forward across the neat writing looking for some stutter in the message, some sign that it wasn't all set in concrete, that it hadn't all been decided.

But it had. In a moment of temper I screwed the letter into a ball.

I hope we can still stay friends. I'd written the exact same words to Joey Hooper just the previous day. Now they sat in front of me in Billy's handwriting.

I let my tea go cold and lay down on top of my bed.

22

Facing the Truth

My dad opened the door of Billy's house almost before I knocked on it. I'd rung ahead on my mobile to make sure he was in. He'd been cooking his meal and took me into the kitchen and made me sit down and drink a cup of tea. There was a strong smell of garlic and herbs. The back door was open and I could see the garden, slightly overgrown. I remembered then that I'd told Billy I would mow the lawn from time to time and I'd completely forgotten to do it. There was the noise of barking dogs and children playing. I wondered what time it was in Africa – just a few hours ahead of England, Billy had told me. For him it might even be dark. He would be hearing the sounds of animals; not cars or radios or next door's TV.

"Patsy, I can't make this right for you. The end of a relationship is always a tough thing."

I nodded my head. Actually I felt curiously detached from it. The skin round my eyes felt tight and dry from where I'd been crying and I had several bunched-up tissues in my bag, but apart from that there was no big gaping wound.

"When you told me he'd gone abroad for a year I assumed that you'd both decided on time apart from each other. Otherwise why would he have gone? Why would you have let him go?"

I didn't answer because I thought he had a point. At the time I was sure we weren't saying goodbye. Maybe that was what I had wanted to think.

"Being apart," my dad said, "it's the worst thing for a relationship."

He turned back to his cooking and half-heartedly stirred some vegetables around. I looked at his shoulders twitching slightly and thought of my mum in London and him in Liverpool. If my mum had gone with him would they still be married now? Should I have gone to Africa with Billy? Would that have made a difference?

"It's the fact that you part, rather than the parting, that breaks the relationship down. Believe me, I've given it a lot of thought over the last fifteen years."

I looked at him and saw something completely new. He was a forty-five-year-old man who'd given up his home and job; he had no partner and only one distant child. My dad was lonely.

"Do you want some of this?" he said, holding out the pan.

"Go on then," I said, forcing a smile.

The food was good, and after eating quietly we began to talk about his hotel in Crete and his plans for the future. He was only in London for another week, he said, then it was off to Greece to meet some architects and builders. It was a fairly typical father-daughter occasion; I'd gone to him with my problems, and I'd ended up feeling sorry for him and talking about his plans for his future.

About seven I decided to go home. I intended to drop by Sherman Street and see if Mr White could corroborate Frank Tully's story about Dixon picking him up. I hoped I might see Alice. I had Harry's letter in my bag and an awful lot of questions to ask.

Truthfully, I was feeling pretty half-hearted about the whole thing. Billy's news had knocked the stuffing out of me and I was only going through the motions of investigating. I had no real *feeling* for it. Either Alice Tully had murdered Melanie or she hadn't. I had a heavy feeling that we weren't going to get much further than that.

Mr White looked surprised to see me. For once I couldn't hear his dogs barking from inside the house.

"I'm sorry to bother you," I said. "I was just wondering if you could confirm something for me."

"No bother at all, my dear," he said, patting down his bow tie.

Just then I noticed a blue van pull into a parking space across the way. There was a sticker on the back window and it looked like Harry Smith's.

In a rushed voice I asked Mr White about the day of the murder. Had he spoken to Frank Tully at all? All the while I kept my eye on the blue van. I could make out two figures in it. Alice Tully and Harry Smith. How brass-necked could they be? Driving right up in front of Alice's house.

Mr White took for ever to answer. I wondered whether his sister was in. She was certainly the more talkative of the two.

Yes, he said, ever so slowly. He had seen Mr Tully. About two, it was. He was on his way in from a walk with the dogs and Mr Tully was on his way out somewhere. He couldn't be exactly sure because there was this horrible dog in a car parked by the pavement. As soon as it saw his Yorkies it went berserk, barking and scratching at the window. He thought that the owner of the car was out on the pavement trying to calm the dog down.

He was confirming what Frank Tully had told me. I glanced over at the stationary van as Mr White was speaking.

Wait, he went on. Now that he thought about it, the man wasn't standing by the car, he was coming out of the Tully's garden. He might have even been coming out of the house. He couldn't be completely sure. A lot of his attention had been taken by the barking dog.

Oh? I said, looking back at the old man. There was the tiniest hint of impatience in my voice.

Very possibly the man had just visited the house

and was coming out. Mr White looked thoughtful. Perhaps he should have mentioned that to the police.

Right, I grimaced. It wasn't clear at all. Frank Tully said Dixon hadn't been in the house, Mr White implied that he might have been.

From the corner of my eye I noticed Alice standing beside the blue van. She smiled and beckoned to me. I was impatient to speak to her so I said goodbye and thank you to Mr White. The old man closed the door quietly.

"We need to talk to you," Alice said, when I reached the van.

I pulled the letter Sue Tully had given me out of my bag.

"About this?" I said, expecting Alice to flinch.

"And other things," she said, her expression only a little shamefaced.

We went to the café at the edge of the forest where Joey and I had sat just a few days before. Harry Smith, avoiding my eyes all the time, went up and bought three cups of tea. I sat on the wooden bench looking at Alice. All the while she was fiddling with her hair or her neck or one of a new pair of earrings that she was wearing.

"You lied to me," I said.

"I know," she answered, "I'm sorry. I know you were trying to help me."

Harry Smith put the cups on the table and sat beside Alice and across from me. I found myself avoiding looking at him. He had lied through his teeth and strung his wife and his two girlfriends along. I had no sympathy for him at all.

"We've found something important out," Alice said, nodding at Harry for confirmation.

I ignored her enthusiasm. I was still angry with her.

"Did you kill Melanie to keep her from telling people about her affair with Harry?" I said it straight to Alice, as though Harry wasn't there.

"No, I didn't. Me and Harry had nothing to do with it."

"Start at the beginning," Harry Smith said, addressing himself to Alice. It seemed that he couldn't look me in the eye either. She gave a heavy sigh.

"A lot of the stuff I told you about me and Harry was true. I did meet him when he was giving leaflets out at my school, I did go to FAST meetings with him, I did go to the dogfight."

"And you got involved with him?"

"Only after that night of the fight."

"I'm surprised he had the time and energy. He had a wife and a girlfriend."

"No. It wasn't like that," he said, finally looking straight at me. "Bernice and me, we hadn't been close for over a year."

"That's not what she said."

"And Melanie, that was just a flirtation. Nothing, I swear, nothing happened between us."

"Apart from a few kisses and cuddles," I said, remembering his words.

Alice looked down at the table. Harry's love life was obviously an embarrassment to her.

"The point is that I fell in love with Alice. We were going to wait until Alice had done her A levels and then be together, except..."

"Except that Melanie was threatening to tell."

"Harry came round on that Saturday to tell me that Melanie had found out about him and me. She was going to go to the police, she said. She was going to create an enormous fuss."

"So you killed her?"

"Don't be ridiculous," Harry Smith said.

I stiffened at his tone. I'd had enough of talking to them. I was about to get up and go when I noticed Alice's wrists. The red line that had circled her arm had gone dark and purple. I remembered the cellar and the feeling I had had that we were never going to get out.

"What about the abduction? Was that a lie as well?"

Alice looked genuinely shocked.

"You think I locked myself up?"

I closed my eyes for a moment and remembered the stairwell when the light had snapped off and the sound of heavy footsteps had been behind me. The man, whoever it had been, had grabbed a lump of my hair. He'd said one word, *Bitch*, and there'd been this funny smell, sweet and heavy, coming from him.

"I spent two nights on my own in that cellar. You think I was pretending?"

"You told me he did it," I said flatly.

"No, I didn't say it was Harry. I said I thought it might be FAST. I knew they had found out about me taking off my mask at the dogfight."

"Once Alice got charged with the murder the people from FAST were very jittery," Harry said. "I kept getting phone calls telling me to keep an eye on her. They didn't know that she and I were involved. Look, I didn't even know she had been abducted until you told me. We were avoiding seeing each other. In case…"

"In case anyone put two and two together," I said, my mind so firmly on the same track that I hardly noticed Alice's agitation.

"Listen to me." Alice put her arm across the table on to my hand and held it firmly, as if by doing that she could stop me from talking. "Don't you think it's funny that my stepsister is murdered and then a week or so later I am abducted? Don't you think there's a link there somewhere?"

"You mean that someone wanted *both* of you dead?"

"Why not?"

It was a possibility that neither I nor Rosa had seriously considered.

"That arsenic. It was there in the food. If I'd felt like lunch Melanie and I would both be dead."

"But who would want that?" I said.

Alice began to shift around in her seat. She looked pleased with herself. Even Harry had begun to smile.

"This afternoon I got Harry to drive me out to Abbeyfield. I wanted to see the place in daylight. I know it's only a matter of time before I go to the police with all of this. I wanted to go back there and see where I'd been imprisoned. We had a look at the village and then we went to the farm. When we got out of the car everything looked familiar."

"You had been there before," I said.

"Not just to me. Everything looked familiar to Harry."

I was puzzled.

"We walked around, and then we both realized. Birch Farm was where the dogfight had been. Harry had followed directions from one of the other lads when we drove there. He had no idea where it was. When we walked round it we both recognized the shapes of buildings, the size of the yard, the old machinery that we'd stood on by the barn. They were there, Patsy. It was the farm where we broke up the dogfight."

"The dogfight," I said, echoing Alice's words.

"I took my mask off. Someone must have recognized me, maybe seen me around. Perhaps they were getting their own back; perhaps they linked me with Harry and FAST and maybe saw Melanie at the Pet Sanctuary. I think we were both meant to die from that arsenic."

I had a picture in my head of Alice standing in the dark yard between the farm buildings, her balaclava by her side, her face and mouth screwed up with nausea. Somewhere in the shadows someone saw her who recognized her. A heavy-set man with a lot to lose if anyone found out that he was involved in illegal abuse of and cruelty to animals.

Why kill Melanie though? She had nothing to do with it. Then it hit me. It was as if it was in mile-high letters, in neon lights, hanging off the back of an aeroplane. We had all missed it, yet it was staring us in the face. Melanie had never been the intended victim.

"Alice, you should go straight to the police."

"Patsy!" Alice looked crestfallen. "You have to believe me. I didn't kill Melanie."

"I do believe you. Only I think you've got one thing wrong. I don't think that food was meant for Melanie at all. I think it was meant for you. Some-body at that dogfight recognized you and couldn't be sure that you hadn't recognized them. They tried to poison you, and when they got the wrong person they abducted you and left you in that cellar to die."

Alice's mouth was open as though she was about to argue.

"Alice, whoever is responsible for this has tried to kill you twice. Don't wait around. Go to the police."

Third time lucky, I was thinking, but I didn't say it.

23

Office Work

At NEWS TALK the next morning Rosa was furious.

"I've just had a phone call from my contact in the police!" she said, her voice carrying right across the room.

I hadn't even made it as far as her office.

"I can explain," I said, keeping my head up high and my shoulders straight.

"You'd better."

She turned her back on me and walked off. Everyone in the room was looking up from their desks. A couple of the girls I had got to know gave me looks of sympathy, the others just rolled their eyes at each other.

I wasn't upset. For the first time since the case began I felt in control of things. Instead of wading through a muddle of information and different stories, making sure that Rosa's precious programme was safe, I could now see clearly the way ahead. I'd even put aside my personal problems and worries. Billy was gone and there was nothing I could do about it. There was, however, something I could do about the case.

Right from the start Alice had been in danger and none of us had seen it. She had got the food out of the fridge and had planned to eat it. Melanie had come home and after a row had had the food herself; maybe out of spite she had demanded it for her own lunch. Whoever had spiked the food had shoved the glass container in one of the bags that hung up by the door. It just happened to be Alice's.

It wasn't Alice and it wasn't Harry, but it must have been someone who had access to the house, even if only for a moment or two.

The person I had in mind was Robert Dixon; but not for the reasons that Rosa suspected him.

He had been in the Tullys' house, I was sure. Mr White thought he had seen him coming out, even though most of his attention had been taken away by the barking dog in the BMW. Perhaps Dixon had only been in the house for a few moments. *Hurry up*, Frank Tully might have said, *my daughter's upstairs and she's just about to have her lunch*.

Why hadn't Frank Tully told the police? Because he was convinced Dixon had nothing to do with the murder and because he didn't want to expose his relationship with him while the discussions about the luxury apartments were going on.

It was my belief that Robert Dixon wasn't worried about any financial scandal. It was simply impossible to prove; the kind of thing that went on all the time, in most government offices. What if he had been involved in an illegal dogfight though? He always had a snarling dog in the back of his car. He lived in Essex, not far from Abbeyfield and Birch Farm. He was a respectable builder. It wouldn't do for him to be exposed as someone who enjoyed seeing animals tearing each other to bits.

It had been a while since the dogfight. Maybe Alice had seen Dixon and her father together. Possibly Dixon had thought that she'd recognized him, remembered him from the dogfight. It was all conjecture; a story I had imagined in my head. How true it was I didn't know. Neither did I know if we would be able to prove any of it. There was precious little evidence; that had been the whole problem from the beginning.

Except that the abduction had been another serious attempt to get rid of Alice. Whoever had masterminded it must have been confident that they would succeed. They had thought that they would go back to Birch Farm a couple of weeks after leaving Alice there and find a dead girl curled in the corner of the cellar. Problem solved, no one any the wiser. This plan fell apart when I found the farm.

My hope was that with Rosa's help we could go to

Dixon's offices, and those of Crown Brokers, and see if we could link the van insurance in some way to Dixon or one of his associates. The person who hired the van said he was insured with Crown Brokers. Could Dixon's business interests have any link with this company? The farm itself hadn't been lived in for years. Had Dixon heard about it through his building and redeveloping interests?

"You've got a lot of explaining to do," Rosa said, sitting down heavily on her desk chair. "My police informant tells me that they've had Alice Tully down at the station for most of the night. Apparently you told her to go and make a clean breast of everything."

"I did."

"You didn't think to ring me? To ask me about it?"

I didn't answer her. I had thought about ringing her but I knew what the result would have been. Rosa would have wanted to avoid the police; to get Alice on tape, to hold the story back for her programme. I was past worrying about the radio station. I was more concerned about Alice's safety.

"Now we won't be able to interview her. Now that she's made a statement we won't be able to use her story for the programme. You've thrown away two weeks of my time and work, and I don't appreciate it."

"She is in danger, Rosa. Someone has tried to kill her twice!"

"What do you mean? It was *Melanie* Tully who died!"

I went through it all, telling the story as I thought

it might have happened. She stopped me a couple of times to ask questions but mostly she was silent. When I'd finished she sat for a moment and then spoke.

"We have no actual evidence against Robert Dixon."

"If we go to Crown Brokers we might find a link."

"Then the police will arrest Robert Dixon and my programme about financial corruption will be finished as well."

"But Rosa, if he poisoned Melanie Tully and tried to kill Alice?"

Rosa was standing up, fiddling about with papers on her desk. Her face was long, her lips pulled tightly across her teeth. I kept talking.

"Think what a scoop it would be. *Top Journalist Exposes Murderer*. We're almost there, Rosa. Don't drop it when we're this close to a result."

I held my fingers up like tiny tongs to show just how close we were. She gave me one of her disdainful looks. Then she pulled all her hair to the back of her neck and held it there for a minute.

"I've no intention of dropping it," she finally said, letting her hair swing forward. "Mainly because of this."

She held a piece of paper up to me. It was a photocopy of a letter from Dixon Enterprises to the council, requesting planning permission to build retirement homes on a two-acre site on Friar Lane, Abbeyfield, Essex.

I didn't say anything. I remembered driving along the country lane on my way to Birch Farm and passing a group of empty houses with a redevelopment sign in front of them.

"I've looked up the map references," she said. "The land he wants to build on is adjacent to Birch Farm. Far too many coincidences; Crown Brokers, Birch Farm, Dixon Enterprises, they're all tripping over each other. Come on, let's go and see the man himself."

The office block was just off the High Road in Ilford. We took the lift to the fourth floor. As we walked up to Dixon Enterprises Rosa hooked her thumb to the left and I saw the offices of Crown Brokers. The company had opaque glass doors each with the gold crown logo on it. A couple of people pushed the doors open and came out as we passed. A cacophony of noise escaped with them; phones ringing, printing machines, a variety of voices talking loudly to make themselves heard.

Dixon's company was a smaller place altogether. A single wooden door with a tiny gold plaque with the words *Dixon Enterprises* on it. It was almost as though it didn't want to be noticed.

We pressed on the intercom and Rosa gave her name. The door buzzed open and we found ourselves in a tiny reception area. It was a room with a low ceiling and a row of chairs for visitors to sit in. A brown-haired woman with pink-tinted glasses was sitting at a computer monitor. The place was hushed and the woman looked slightly startled to see us.

"Hello again," she said, smiling uncertainly at Rosa.

"Hi, I was wondering if Mr Dixon was available for a few minutes?" Rosa said, flashing an even bigger smile back.

"I'll just check for you. Please, take a seat."

We sat down on the chairs opposite her desk. The receptionist had the receiver up to her ear and then turned her head away from us slightly as she spoke quietly into it. Rosa nudged me and I looked up at the wall and saw a large photograph of Mr Dixon, squatting down beside an alsatian. He was holding a cup. Underneath were the words, *Winner of Class: Essex Finals*. It was very like the manic dog that I had seen in the back of his car.

Perhaps Mr Dixon was well known in dog circles; a breeder or a show enthusiast. Could it be that he was also involved in dogfights?

"OK," the receptionist said, more loudly, "I'll tell them."

She replaced the telephone with great care and then took her glasses off before turning to us.

"Mr Dixon's with a client at the moment. He could see you in about ten minutes?"

"I'll wait," Rosa said, doggedly smiling.

The woman began to fiddle about with her computer. Ten minutes was a long time to wait. I was feeling agitated, my knees moving up and down with impatience. After a couple of moments I stood up and brushed down my clothes.

"I'll just get a breath of fresh air," I said and Rosa looked quizzically at me.

I walked out of the tiny office and into the corridor. Just then one of the lifts opened and a woman with a basket of sandwiches stepped out. She was looking at a piece of paper in her hand.

"Crown Brokers?" she asked.

I smiled and pointed to the sign which she would have noticed a moment or so later anyway. Then I walked after her and held one of the double doors open while she manoeuvred herself into the reception area. I followed her in, not quite sure what I was going to do once I was in there.

The receptionist was a young man and he was sitting on one side of a glass partition. On the other side the office stretched back behind him. He was speaking to someone on the telephone and hardly looked at the sandwich woman as he waved her on into the office itself. I followed after her.

The office was about the size of a classroom. There were about ten workstations, most of which seemed to have people sitting at them. In-between were little alleyways cordoned off by screens or filing cabinets or small islands of lush plants. A lot of these workstations had been customized, with photos of family or film stars or cartoons cut out from newspapers and stuck on any available surface.

A couple had those silly sayings like *You don't have to be mad to work here, but it helps!*

I had some half-brained idea that I would find out whether Dixon Enterprises did business with Crown Brokers. But once I was there, standing awkwardly in the middle of the office, I had no idea how I was going to go about it. I couldn't just walk up to anyone and say, *Do you do business with Dixon Enterprises?* So I just followed the sandwich woman as she wove among the workstations and handed out triangles of food.

I wasn't downhearted. There was a link, I was sure. It was just a matter of getting to the information. Dixon would need insurance for his company workers and vehicles; perhaps he used the company closest to his offices.

I wondered if I could find the man I telephoned when I was at VANLOAN. It would be a good start and a way of introducing myself. I remembered then that he had had a heavy cough, and I wondered if I might be able to hear him above the sounds of chatter and tapping of keyboards. I listened for a moment, but heard nothing. Then something caught my eye.

It was a workstation about three metres away from me. Above it were the words *Company Insurance A-M*. There was no one sitting there but the computer screen-saver was on with the words CROWN BROKERS: FORGET THE REST INSURE WITH THE BEST sliding across it. I left the sandwich woman and walked towards it. I decided to say that I was a temp from Dixon's office and I'd popped by to pick up copies of his recent accounts. I didn't know if it was a feasible request but I thought it would just get us talking. If the person said, *We don't have a Dixon on our books*, then that would be that.

I didn't believe that would be the answer. I was guessing that Dixon did all of his business with one of the brokers in the office and in return he had asked for a favour; insurance cover for the blue Ford van. I imagined the builder making up a story: *I need to hire a van under a different name; it's nothing illegal, just private business. You can let me borrow a licence and some fake insurance, can't you, old boy?* Maybe he gave a little mock salute as he said it.

A girl of about eighteen was at the next computer. She had a pencil in her mouth and was typing with two fingers, her face screwed up with concentration.

"Excuse me," I said. I was about to ask her about Dixon when I stopped in surprise.

The side of the filing cabinet next to the computer was covered from top to toe in pictures of dogs. There were lots of Yorkies and spaniels and even a couple of poodles, bows on their heads and their tails looking like pompoms. In the middle of it all was a picture of a man and an older lady.

It was Miss White, the Tully's next-door neighbour. Beside her was Mr White wearing a sleeveless pullover and a check shirt. For once there was no bow-tie.

"Is this the man who works here?" I said to the girl on the computer.

"Mr White? He's not here at the moment. He has a week's leave."

Mr White, the man next door to the Tullys', was an insurance broker. I remembered that his sister said he was working on his computer on the day that Melanie was poisoned. I was confused. It wasn't what I wanted to hear at all. I had already worked out what had happened.

I stood for a minute, perplexed. *Mr White, the next-door neighbour.* The dog-lover; the man who had his own pet cemetery. I remembered his kitchen wall covered in photographs of dogs. His award as *Star Fund-raiser 1998.* His sister had said he worked in insurance; indeed, on the day of Melanie's death he'd been working at home. They'd owned eleven dogs, Miss White had said. They'd had names like Lolly, Bertie and Postie.

"Can I help you with something?" the girl with the pencil in her mouth said.

Birch Farm came into my head then. I remembered the sign outside it, *Birch Farm and Kennels.* The farm hadn't just been for agriculture, it had also been a home for dogs. Could Mr White have known about the empty farmhouse? Had the Whites used the kennels to board their dogs while they'd gone on holiday?

"Do you need something?" I heard the girl's voice. She had stopped typing and was looking at me in a concerned way.

Had Mr White known that the farm was closed? That it was uninhabited? Could he have used the buildings for the dogfight and later for the abduction? I turned away from the pictures and walked along the alleyway towards the doors of the office. I was remembering the cellar stairwell at Birch Farm, taking the steps carefully and quickly, optimistic about rescuing Alice. The light had simply vanished. One minute it hung like yellow fog in the air and the next minute the blackness had swallowed it up. The footsteps on the stairs behind, rushed and heavy. The man's hand on my hair, his mouth close to my ear; *Bitch*, he'd said and I'd smelled a sweet pungent smell from him.

Pear drops. *My brother's favourite*, Miss White had said. The man who had pushed me into the cellar had smelled of pear drops.

It hadn't been Dixon at all. I'd been wrong. The answer had been there, just metres from the Tully's kitchen.

"Are you all right?" Rosa said when I got back into Dixon's offices.

"We need to go, right now," I said.

The receptionist with the pink glasses stopped working and looked at us.

"Where?" Rosa said. "I've not seen Dixon yet!"

"It's not him," I said, between my teeth.

"Where are we going?" she asked, rushing behind me to catch up.

"To visit some OAPs," I said.

24

Family Loyalty

Miss White answered the door. She smiled when she saw me. Then she looked expectantly at Rosa.

"This is my colleague Rosa Perks," I said, bending down to pat one of the dogs. "Is your brother at home?"

"He's out, I'm afraid. Why don't you come in? He'll be back soon. You can have a cup of tea while you wait."

We went in behind the old lady. In the hallway were some suitcases and a couple of holdalls.

"We're going to Hastings for a few days," Miss White said. "It's so rare my brother has any time off we thought we'd take a break."

I wondered how Miss White would react when she found out that her brother was a murderer. And then

I thought, *Does she already know?* She wouldn't be the first person to protect a close loved one. She was walking quite slowly up the hall and both Rosa and I were taking tiny steps so as not to overtake her. How would she cope alone when her brother went to prison?

In the kitchen she chatted on while she made the tea. She asked Rosa about her job and Rosa, while fending off the advances of the dogs, described it. I could hear Miss White saying, "How interesting, how very interesting!" All the while I was looking at my watch wondering when her brother would get in. My eyes flicked over the wall of photographs, the portraits of dogs they had had, their heads tipped at an angle, their eyes as black as coal, looking lovingly at the camera. How could Mr White have got involved in something so cruel as dogfighting?

I heard the front door open.

"That's Mr White," the old lady said, with a smile.

The kitchen door opened and Mr White came in. He looked completely different. He was wearing a tracksuit with a zip-up jacket and looked about ten years younger. I also noticed, for the first time, the breadth of his shoulders and how solid his neck looked. He was a strong man, I could see that now. Before, in his bow-tie and pullovers, he'd looked old and weedy.

He glanced at both of us for only a second and then looked hard and long at his sister.

"These two ladies have come to have a word, dear," she said, her voice full of false cheer.

At that moment I was sure that Miss White knew about the murder.

"Mr White," I said, in a friendly voice, "I believe you work for Crown Brokers? Only I spoke to you on the phone just a couple of days ago to ask you about a Mr Raymond? He hired a van and gave his insurance details as…"

Mr White put his hand up for me to stop.

"You don't need to say any more," he said, "I know you've found out about the farm and the dog-fight and the girl. You can call the police. I'll make a full confession."

There was silence as these words sunk in. Then Miss White spoke in an authoritative voice, her words filling the small kitchen.

"Larry, this is silly. Don't say another word. These girls have no evidence."

Rosa and I both looked as though we'd been slapped.

"I'm sorry, but we do," Rosa snapped back.

"The girl next door, Alice? She saw me at a dog-fight in Essex. I was afraid she would go to the police so I tried to poison her. Her sister ate the food by mistake. That made matters even worse. I was sure it would all come out then so I took the girl away and left her in a cellar. " Mr White said it all calmly.

"Larry, no…" Miss White said.

"She was never meant to come out of that cellar alive." He pointed at me. "I believe I have you to thank for that,"

Every word he said was crisp and clear with not a jot of emotion. I felt chilled by the detachment with which he talked about the lives of two young girls.

"Call the police. Here, use this," he said, pulling a mobile out of his tracksuit trousers. He laid it on the table and sat back, a look of resignation on his face.

"I'll use my own," Rosa said and started to jab at the numbers on her phone. It wasn't a 999 call, I knew that. She was ringing her contact at the station. He, whoever he was, would make the arrest and get the credit. It was Rosa's way of paying her dues for all the information he had got from her.

"Where did you get the poison?" I said.

"Pesticide. A contact of mine in the industry got it." Mr White waved his hand dismissively as though it had been the easiest thing in the world.

Miss White had sat herself down in a chair, her face suddenly drawn and looking her age. She was absentmindedly pampering the dogs, one of whom had jumped up on her lap and was licking her neck. The others, round her ankles, were giving little indignant barks. She picked the one on her lap up and placed it on the floor with the others. Then she got up and walked to the sink. I was reminded then of the first day I had seen her, when she gave me the sweet. Her dogs had liked me, she said. *Usually they bark at everyone, my dear. Even my brother. They're only quiet for me.*

I heard Rosa's voice talking quietly to her contact

at the police station, giving the address and telling them not to come with their sirens blaring.

No one had heard Miss White's dogs barking on the day that Melanie was poisoned. Yet if Mr White had gone out into the back garden and slipped through the fence wouldn't they have barked? From inside even? I had heard them barking from the end of the garden path. Not even Miss White could keep them all quiet all of the time. In my head something nasty was uncurling itself. Was Larry White's confession the truth or was he covering up for someone else?

"So after you put the poison in the food you put the container in the bin and came back," I said, casually.

Rosa, still talking on her mobile, looked at me quizzically. Miss White had picked up the dogs' drinking bowl and was filling it at the tap.

"That's right," he said, "I got rid of it."

"In the bin, under the sink," I said, making a guess as to the whereabouts of the bin.

He nodded. "I said, yes, didn't I?"

Rosa's phone call had ended and she was looking at both of us. Miss White turned around and put the bowl on the floor. It was as if she wasn't really listening any more. Larry White hadn't put the poison in the food after all. It had been his sister, the kindly old lady who cared so much for her animals.

In my mind's eye I saw Miss White walking slowly but steadily up the garden. Maybe she had the poison in the pocket of her apron, next to the sweets she carried about with her. I imagined her going into the kitchen and sprinkling it into the dish. If someone had come she would probably have made some reasonable excuse. *One of the dogs ran away dear, I was just fetching him back.* On her way out she had tucked the glass container in one of the bags.

Larry White was looking at me. It was as if he could read my mind.

"I did it. I poisoned the girl. It was me."

But it wasn't him. It was Miss White, his sister.

At the local police station Miss White was taken to one interview room by a WPC. Larry White was taken to another. Both of them refused to answer questions until they had their family solicitor present. Rosa stayed for the whole time and I went on home. About five she called by my house. She looked tired but happy. Her contact had told her the details and she had noted them down. Once the trial was over she would be able to use it all to make a programme about it.

"And not just for the radio," she told me excitedly. "I've got a friend who has a production company and he's thinking of filming it!"

When she'd calmed down I made her a cup of tea and she got out her reporter's notepad and told me the story of what had happened.

Miss White, whose name was Mabel, was seventeen years older than her brother. The old lady had already told me this. Her mother had had the boy when she was in her forties and didn't have much time for babies. Mabel looked after him as a child and continued to do so when he was an adult. When his wife had died of cancer some twenty years before, Mabel White had moved in with her brother. The two of them lived together in Sherman Street. She had her dogs and he had his. It was only after she'd lived with him for about ten years that she'd found out about the dogfights. Even then she had made excuses for her brother. *Men are different to women. They are naturally aggressive. The dogfights are a way of letting that aggression go.* She appeared to have little sympathy for the dogs. *It's only natural for some breeds*, she'd said to the Detective Inspector, *they're only once removed from wolves, after all.*

She managed to live with her brother's vice. Between the two of them they felt they made up for it with the charity work and the fund-raising. They had a high public standing because of the work they did for animals. All that would have been destroyed if word had got out about the dogfights. Her brother made her the pet cemetery. *We only buried our own dogs there!* she had said. The other dogs, the ones who had died fighting, she couldn't account for.

When Larry White came home on the night he'd seen Alice at the dogfight he'd told his sister immediately. At first the pair decided to brazen it out. Alice might not have recognized Mr White. They might have been worrying for nothing. Indeed, after a week or two when nothing had happened, both of them thought the matter was forgotten.

Except that Miss White began to notice Alice looking out of the front bedroom window. When she looked she always seemed to catch the young woman's eye. Then she saw Alice meeting the young man in the van, the one with the FAST sticker on the back. Mabel White knew about FAST. She'd looked it up on the internet when her brother had been out. As time went on Miss White convinced herself that Alice was only biding her time and that she would report her beloved brother to the police.

Larry White knew nothing about the poison. It was only when Melanie's body was discovered and the news circulated that his sister told him what she had done. He was appalled, he said. He was also determined to shield his sister from discovery. That's why he took Alice away. That's why he put her into the cellar. *I couldn't kill a girl with my bare hands*, he'd said, *but if I left her there and went back and found her dead it wouldn't seem like I was responsible.*

Rosa Perks closed her pad and sat back looking pleased with herself. She was wearing a black dress with a white cardigan and white sandals. I wanted to ask her why she wore black and white all the time. I couldn't though. It was the kind of question that was outside the bounds of our working relationship.

Me? I didn't see life in crisp black and white lines. I preferred the uncertainty of colour. It made things more interesting, if a little more messy.

25

Goodbyes

I drove my dad to the airport. We were far too early for his plane so after he checked in we went and sat at a coffee bar. He was looking crisp yet casual in jeans and a loose open-necked shirt. Over his arm he had some expensive-looking hand luggage and a briefcase which he said held all his papers. He had a large black coffee that came in a glass mug with two tiny biscuits by its side. I had a tea and a Danish pastry that was the size of a dinner plate and seemed to be covered in syrup. It tasted good and he rolled his eyes at me as I ate it.

"Don't you worry about your weight?" he said.

"Nope!" I said between mouthfuls.

I knew that he watched what he ate. That morning I'd cleared Billy's fridge out as he'd been closing windows and doors; low fat milk and cheese, tofu, pasta, organic vegetables. My dad's digestive system hadn't seen a bag of chips for many years.

"I'm feeling nervous about this," he said, tidying up his tickets and sandwiching them inside his passport.

"Flying?"

"No, starting afresh. At my age."

"You'll be fine," I said, not really knowing whether he would or not.

"You'll come and visit?"

I nodded and he drank some of his coffee, giving a sideways glance to a woman who was sitting reading a newspaper at the next table. She was blonde and glamorous and her scarlet nails matched her strappy sandals and shoulder bag. She looked up for a millisecond and caught his eye. Then she returned to her paper. I wondered if she was his type.

The last time I had been in an airport was to see Billy off to Africa. I had thought that I would be back there, one year on, with a placard that said *WELCOME BACK!* but it didn't look like that was going to happen. Never mind about putting on weight from eating cakes, I felt about a stone heavier with the disappointment of it all.

"What will happen to the old couple?" my dad said.

Rosa Perks had kept me informed. She'd taken to ringing me up and idly chatting for a few moments before she got down to business. I wasn't sure whether I liked the attention or not.

"Mabel White has been charged with murder and her brother has been charged with unlawful abduction and attempted murder. They're both on remand at the moment, pending medical reports."

"They surely won't send a woman of her age to trial?" my dad said.

He only sounded mildly interested. At the same time as asking he was craning his neck to look at the TV monitor in the far corner of the lounge. I could see the words DEPARTURES INFORMATION in the distance.

"What difference does her age make? She killed a teenage girl."

"I suppose so," he said, picking up one of his tiny biscuits and dunking it into his coffee.

I saw him up to the Departure Lounge turnstile. He was looking nervous and gave me a hug that lasted longer than usual. I watched as he finally disappeared into a crowd of people heading for the security check gate. I was confused by how unaffected I felt by his departure.

What had I hoped for? That I would weep and sob; that I would try and persuade him to stay and live in London? He was my dad and I cared about him, but he hadn't been around much and I didn't have a great hunger for his company. All the same, I was glad that he was doing something positive with his life. Maybe Crete would make him happy.

When I got home I could hear the sound of drums thudding through my front door. I opened it to a blast of rock music that made me put my fingers in my ears. I felt immediately irritated and couldn't imagine why the music was so loud. I tutted to myself and said, "Honestly!" as I closed the door behind me. I called out to my mum but couldn't make myself heard above the beat. I walked swiftly down the hallway to where the sound was coming from and angrily threw the kitchen door open.

My mum and Gerry had their backs to me. They were both cutting up vegetables and *dancing* at the same time. Gerry was in his newly acquired track-suit bottoms and my mum was wearing shorts and a T-shirt. In a moment of astonishment I was lost for words. They were both moving around to the music and neither of them had heard me come in. Gerry suddenly turned in my direction and appeared to be playing an invisible guitar. My mum, using the potato peeler as an imaginary microphone, began to sing at the top of her voice.

When they saw me they both stopped. The three of us looked at each other as the heavy music played on in the background. It was Mum who laughed first, then Gerry.

"Will you turn this music down!" I said.

My words started angrily but halfway through I began to see the ludicrousness of the situation and I started to giggle as well. My mum slipped around me and went into the living room to turn off the hi-fi. The sudden silence seemed heavy with echoes of the music that had stopped playing. When she came back into the kitchen she put her hand on my shoulder.

"Your dad get away all right?"

"Fine," I said.

"Cup of tea, Pats?" Gerry said, scratching the bit of stomach that was hanging over the waistband of his joggers.

"Go on then," I said, plonking myself down on a chair.

"A man on a motorbike delivered this for you," my mum said, handing me an envelope. Above my address were the words *By Hand, Patsy Kelly, Private Investigator*. I tore it open. Inside was a note from Rosa.

Great news. The programme is on. You're going to be on TV!

Regards, Rosa!

Trust Rosa to send it by motorbike courier. I found myself smiling anyway.

I'd wanted a change of job but I hadn't been aiming that high.

"What is it?" my mum asked, chewing on a carrot.

"I'm going to be a celebrity!" I said, laughing.

I folded the letter up and put it in my pocket while the both of them looked at me uncertainly. They didn't know how serious I was. But then neither did I.